Stars Over Montana

CLEAN, SECOND CHANCE WESTERN ROMANCE

COWBOYS OF RIVER JUNCTION
BOOK ONE

LUCINDA RACE

Manufactured in the United States of America
First Edition September 2022
Print Edition 978-1-954520-37-0
E-book ISBN 978-1-954520-36-3

Authors Note

Hi and welcome to my world of romance. I hope you love my characters as much I do. So, turn the page and fall in love again.

If you'd like to stay in touch, please join my Newsletter. I release it twice per month with tidbits, recipes and an occasional special gift just for my readers so sign up here: https://lucindarace. com/newsletter/ and there's a free book when you join!

Happy reading...

Chapter One

Grace Star Ranch. The sign was prominently displayed on the wood and iron arch over Annie as she stood and surveyed all that was rolled out in front of her. From the miles of gravel roads to the streams and mountains, the cattle and buildings and even the cowboys were all her responsibility. But this wasn't just any ranch; it was hers now that her beloved Pops left it to her. But who was she kidding? It was only by default since she was the last of the Grace family.

Her gaze followed the long road where it forked to the right, leading to the main house, and the left led to the actual working part of the ranch. She got back in her BMW and sped down the road, kicking up billows of dust in her wake. She smiled as her thoughts turned to Pops. He'd be ticked if he could see how fast she was driving on his beloved land. Out of respect to her late grandfather, she eased back on the gas and drove the rest of the way to the house with nary a puff of dust, let alone a cloud.

Her heart caught in her throat when the house came into view, but that was an understatement. From a humble footprint, it had grown into over seven thousand square feet of home. Pops had designed it so she had her own wing separate from his, but they would have meals and family time together. She stopped again and waited for the lump in her throat to clear. Had it only been two months since she was here and buried the best man she had ever known? The memories of her parents had faded over the years. They had died when she was young, but now she had come home to decide what the future would be for the ranch and all the men and women who worked for Pops. Wait, check that—for her.

She parked under the portico and walked up the wide stone steps and onto the expansive wraparound porch. She dropped her shoulder bag and turned to take in the sweeping views of the land. There was no place on earth like Montana. In the distance she could see the snowcapped mountains and the grass was brilliant green. Grazing cattle dotted the landscape and from here she could see ranch hands on horseback, working at whatever chores were on tap for today. She noticed the barns and bunkhouses were in pristine condition and everywhere there was landscaped grass, it had been mowed recently. She wasn't in Boston anymore.

She inhaled the fresh mountain air deep into her lungs, squared her shoulders, and pushed open the heavy wooden door. The house was quiet except for the faint sounds coming from the back of the house. It had to be Mary, Pops longtime housekeeper. She had been her grandmother Pippa's best friend, and when she died about twelve years ago, Mary took over looking after Pops. Everything came full circle.

"Mary?" She slipped off her lightweight wool

jacket and leather boots—old habits never died. She walked down the hallway in the direction of the muffled sounds.

She eased open the door to Pops' office and stopped on the threshold. Mary was standing on the top rung of a stepladder, dusting the elk horn chandelier. She was afraid to say anything lest she scare the older woman, causing her to fall.

"Don't be hovering in the doorway, child. Come in and hold the ladder for me."

Annie rushed forward and put her foot on the bottom rung to keep the ladder from swaying.

"Mary, what are you doing up there? Couldn't you get one of the hands to come in and help you?"

She looked down with a frown firmly in place. "They've got their own work to do and I wanted to get Pops' office cleaned before you arrived. You've got work to do to keep the ranch running on an even keel and the best place to do that is right there." She thrust her feather duster in the direction of an oversized wooden desk and a well-worn deep-burgundy leather chair that faced a wall of glass. The view was fantastic. Featuring the working ranch, from here she could see the horse and cattle barns and the dining hall for the ranch hands. She smiled, remembering the parties they held there too.

Refocusing on the matter at hand, she said, "You could have fallen and that would have been a fine howdy when I walked in here."

Mary waved a hand. "I've been climbing on this ladder for at least forty years, which is just a few years more than you've walked on this earth." She gave a chuckle. "I'm coming down."

She climbed down and it was easy to see Mary was just as spry as ever.

Annie wrapped her arms around her surrogate grandmother and squeezed her tight. "It's good to see you, Mary."

She rubbed her back. "And you, child. Come with me and let's have some coffee." She eased from Annie's arms. "I made your favorite blondies for a little welcome home treat."

She kissed Mary's cheek. "You're too good to me."

"There's nothing I wouldn't do for the Grace family and that includes baking up tasty treats."

Annie followed Mary from the office. With a last look over her shoulder, she knew Mary was correct. Her butt would be in that chair tomorrow morning to start familiarizing herself with what had been happening in the last fifteen years since she moved over two thousand miles away.

Over coffee Annie caught Mary up on her life. Well, what had been her life up until five days ago.

"You put your stuff in storage, rented your townhouse, and drove across the country?" Mary wiped her fingertips on the forest-green cloth napkin.

"I did. It gave me time to decompress from work."

"Right, your job with the management firm. Did you like analyzing other companies' bottom line?"

"It was interesting to see how people could change a few things and yield a better ROI. But sometimes getting clients to listen was challenging."

"Your grandfather was very proud of your talent in business."

Did she hear a subtle reproach in Mary's voice or was it just her imagination? What if she had stayed to learn how to run the ranch as Pops' right hand? But going to Boston College had been his idea initially; she had wanted to stay after high school. She looked out the front window and her thoughts drifted to Linc. She knew he was out there somewhere, working with the cattle. Did he know he still had her heart? That was part of the reason she was here, to close that door once and for all so she could move on with her life.

Softly, she said, "I hope he was." She looked at Mary over her coffee mug. "Tell me what's been going on around here."

"Calves have been born; fence repairs are going on, and they're getting ready to plant. The usual." She topped off their coffee. "But I suspect Lincoln will fill you in tomorrow."

She felt her eyes go wide. "What do you mean, fill me in?" She had no intention of spending time talking with Linc Cooper about anything.

"Child, he's running the ranch. Pops turned

over the day-to-day to him two years ago. Right after the last time you were here and announced you weren't ready to come home. Well before the funeral, of course. He mentored the boy so that you'd have someone you could trust."

"Mary, he's hardly a boy. Last I looked he was pushing forty."

She arched a brow. "Good to know you still got eyes in that pretty head."

Annie shook her head. "Not like that, so don't go getting any ideas. This is just business."

"I've heard that saying before in those romance movies I like to watch. It's what the girl says right before she tumbles for the handsome hero." She patted Annie's hand. "He's still easy on the eyes too."

"That won't make a bit of difference. You know he broke my heart years ago and there's no forgetting that."

"What I know is you were both too young and you needed to get off this ranch and see the world, live in a city so you'd appreciate the wide-open spaces here."

"I know I had to leave and it was the right

thing to do. Boston is a wonderful old city and I loved everything about it from the harbor to the cobblestone streets in the North End, but this ranch was always my home." Her heart flipped in her chest. Until she made up her mind if she wanted to sell it or let Linc run the place for her and she'd head back to Boston.

"I'm glad to hear that." She pushed back from the table. "You should go get settled. I have a nice supper planned. Your favorites—roast chicken, biscuits, gravy, and carrots."

"What, no pie?"

She wagged a finger and shook her head. "Do you ever remember a night that we didn't have some kind of dessert with dinner? Your Pops insisted that a working man needed a full supper which included dessert." She patted her midsection. "I've been having to eat a lot of dessert on my own the last few months and it shows."

She got up and threw her arms around Mary. "You've always been slender and you're as beautiful as ever." She kissed her cheek. "I'm going to unload the car, and don't you worry, I won't be late for dinner."

"Best not." Her eyes twinkled. "Or no chocolate cream pie for you."

Annie groaned. She was going to have to spend some time working outdoors if Mary was going to be feeding her. "How do you feel about a salad night once or twice a week?"

"You'll rethink that after you start working again." She pointed out the window. "I know you, and there'll be some office time, but you'll want to be working with the animals too." She tapped the middle of Annie's chest. "It's part of who you are."

Annie set her bags on the ground next to the car. It was surprising she was able to get four suitcases in the trunk and the small back seat was jam-packed too. What had she been thinking when she bought the coupe? *That it was perfect for the city. But an SUV would be better out here. Unless she'd head back to the city before winter settled in.*

She yanked on the handles of the two largest bags and she heard, "Let me help you with those."

She didn't have to turn around. She'd know

that voice anywhere; she even heard it in her dreams. Linc.

Slowly she looked into his gold-flecked hazel eyes. There were more crinkles around them from squinting in the sun. It didn't matter how many times she had told him to wear sunglasses; he said his cowboy hat was enough. She could see strands of gray in his dark sideburns and the cleft in his chin was still begging for her fingertips to trace it and then slide to outline his lips. Damn, he was still good-looking enough to make her go weak-kneed. Why couldn't he be one of those guys who didn't age well?

"Linc, what are you doing here?"

He met her steady gaze and seemed to enjoy the way she was looking at him. "I saw the car with Massachusetts plates and figured it had to be you so I came over to be neighborly."

Ha. Neighborly, her fanny. He wanted to poke the bear and see if he could find out what her plans were. He had always been one to want to know what she was thinking even before she did herself.

He took a small bag under each arm and grabbed the two largest roller bags. "You can get the last ones." He nodded in the direction of the back seat. Before she could answer, he was striding up the steps and through the front door.

She grabbed the final bags and hurried to keep up with him, but why did his legs have to be so long and look so good in jeans? With a suppressed laugh, she trailed behind him. She could enjoy the view but the key to surviving this encounter with her old flame was to be frosty. That would quench any embers that might want to catch fire.

By the time she walked inside he was disappearing down the hallway. Of course, he'd remember where her room was; it had a view of the horse barn. When Pops added her wing onto the house, he designed it so she'd be able to keep a close eye on her love, Bowie. She hoped the horse would be thrilled to see her tomorrow.

Linc came back down the hall and took the last two bags from Annie. "I'll get these for you too."

She tried to hang on but gave in when he cocked his head as if questioning why she wouldn't just let go. This was not something worth fighting about. The man had always had a chivalrous streak as wide and long as the Missouri River that ran through this ranch. Some things were just easier, like floating along with the current, but she needed to be careful not to get pulled under.

She entered her old room and it was just as if she still lived here. There was a photo of her parents on the long dresser and one of Pops and Pippa next to it. Much to her chagrin, a picture of her and Linc sat on her nightstand. Why she never put it away all these years was something she didn't want to explain. She eased over and tried to block it. If Linc noticed, he didn't say a word.

"Thanks for carrying my bags."

He gestured to them. "Awful lot of stuff for a short visit. How long are you planning on staying?"

"Not sure yet, but for a while, and you know me. I love my clothes and shoes."

He tipped his hat up and her breath caught. Now she had a good look at his all-seeing eyes. He looked at her as if he wanted to say something, but the words never formed.

"I'll be in the kitchen if you have a minute."

"Sure. I'll be right out."

He left the room and it was like the air had sucked out after him. She needed to wrap her head around being in charge of the ranch. She couldn't afford any more awkward encounters like the one that just happened.

She slid open the glass door and stepped out on the small stone patio. The cool air wafted over her face and she closed her eyes, letting the sun warm her face. *Pops, I promise I'll do my best and somewhere in that big ole desk of yours, I hope you left me a clue as to how I carry on the legacy of Grace Star Ranch.*

When Annie got to the kitchen, Linc had made himself comfortable on a stool and Mary was handing him a mug of coffee and a large wedge of a blondie. *He was right at home, just like when we were kids hanging out in the kitchen, getting an afternoon snack from Pippa and Mary. Maybe this was going to be okay.*

"There you are, Annie. Can I pour you another cup of coffee?"

"No, thank you." She bobbed her head in the direction of the other room.

Mary said, "I need to take care of something so I'll leave you and Linc to catch up."

Annie waited until Mary left the room before saying, "So what's on your mind?"

Chapter Two

Linc sipped his coffee and took his time answering Annie's question. Seeing her looking as beautiful as always was like getting kicked in the middle of his chest by a stallion he was trying to break. She looked the part of what he thought a city girl should look like, thin with curves in all the right places to keep a cowboy warm at night. Her short dark hair was styled and not a lock out of place. Her deep-red lipstick begged him to kiss it off, but of course he wouldn't be kissing her again. That bridge was burned to a crisp. But it was her crystal-blue eyes that held his heart tethered to her. At one time there had been so much love in them, just for him. It had been her last year of college, and he didn't want her to miss all the opportunities life had to offer so he deliberately broke her heart. He snapped out of his trip down memory lane when she spoke.

"I wanted to see how your trip was and make plans for us to talk tomorrow about the ranch. The guys and I want to make sure if you have any changes that we get started on them right away."

Not that she'd want to change much as far as running the business was concerned. It ran like a well-oiled machine. Her grandfather had a firm but light grip on the reins, never too tight to spook anyone. Everyone knew he was ultimately in charge but there was a bit of freedom too. Linc wanted to honor his memory and run the ranch the same way, but he needed to know what Annie's intentions were. Was she sticking around, thinking she could run the place herself and he'd be out of a job? Only time would tell.

She leaned against the counter and studied

him for several long minutes without speaking. He wanted to shift in his seat, but it was like being stared down when he was breaking a horse. It was all a waiting game.

"The trip was uneventful. Five days along interstate ninety was the same as the previous times I've driven it. Thanks for asking."

He didn't have a follow-up question about Boston. Instead, he said, "Will you have time to go over some things tomorrow? Morning or afternoon is fine. I just want to get a handle on what you're thinking for the future."

Her forehead wrinkled and she rubbed the tip of her nose—a telltale sign she wasn't certain what would come next for any of them.

"Sure. Why don't you come over after lunch if that works. Are you still eating at noon sharp?"

"Yup. Quinn gets everything out by noon. Want to come down and meet him? He's new since you were here last." He didn't want to point out that she had missed far too many holidays leaving Pops alone, but he got it. Her job was about numbers and year-end she must have been busy wrapping things up. At least that was the excuse Pops gave him.

"When was he hired?"

"'Bout three years ago now. He's good. The guys like him and he's into clean eating so everyone's cholesterol numbers should have dropped after Buck retired." He gave her a slow smile. "You know how he loved his bacon grease."

She nodded and the easy grin that spread across her face was the real deal, not the plastic version she plastered on when she was merely being polite. "I'm surprised we didn't have more guys with heart conditions after working here."

"You mean like most other ranches in the state." He brushed the cookie crumbs off the counter and got up and rinsed them down the drain. He was so close to her, and she smelled like clean wash on the line. He dropped his eyes and heard her breath catch. He held himself back from lowering his mouth to hers and turned away.

"I can come up around one. You might want to sleep in after your long drive."

She snorted. "When have you ever heard of

me sleeping late?" She shook her head. "Don't answer that. I'm not going to revisit *our past*."

He didn't like how she had put extra emphasis on *our past*. It almost made it sound like she had regrets. Well, he had a few, the biggest being convincing her that he didn't love her. His younger self was an idiot.

"You should take a walk around. We've made some upgrades and there are new calves, and a few mares will be foaling soon. I know how much you love that."

"And Bowie, is she going to have one this year?"

He gave a half nod. "She is. Your grandfather thought it might be the last year we bred her." Now he wondered if it was because he knew Annie would be home. Last year Pops had been given six to twelve months and he got almost twelve. It was as if Bowie foaling was his last gift to Annie.

"Is she doing okay?"

"Like the star she is. But she's huge; it'll be anytime now."

"I'm glad I made it before she gave birth. I had no clue she was this close."

Had she even asked about the horses when she was back for Pops' last days and the funeral? More than likely not since emotions were running high and he was gone in three days after the big decline started. Thankfully Annie had the chance to say her goodbyes.

"Thanks for taking good care of her. She's all I have left of Pops."

"And now her foal." With a gentle touch, he placed a hand on her arm. "You also have the ranch."

She wiped away the tear that slipped down her cheek. "Sorry, it's still a lot to deal with."

He wanted to wrap his arms around her and hold her close, stroke her hair until she realized she wasn't alone. But he was the manager of the ranch and not her family.

He stepped back. "I'm going to head out but if you need something, my cell number is on the counter or there's always the walkie-talkies." He could feel her eyes on him as he walked out the side door.

· · ·

Later that night Linc sat on the porch of his house. It was more of a large cabin but as the ranch manager, he had his own space. His best friend, Clint Goodman, also had his own place. It was a little smaller than this, but he was the foreman now. He'd replaced Linc when Pops promoted him to manager.

He loved this time of night just when the darkness wrapped around the ranch with the stars making their appearance in the endless inky sky. How did Annie survive in a city with all the lights and sounds, never to see the vast expanse of wonder? He'd go mad if he couldn't see this every night. Even on the nights there were clouds, he knew the stars were there, waiting to show up again. He propped his boots on the railing as he listened to the silence.

A movement from off to the left side caused him to sit up straighter. The bunkhouse was to the right. There shouldn't be any mountain lions this close to the house since there were plenty of animals to hunt and the bears should still be near the rivers catching fish to fill their empty bellies. The moonlight cast a glow over Annie. It was obvious she was making her way to the horse barn. She was going to see Bowie, her first love.

He debated if he should follow her or give her space, but common sense overruled him and he got to his feet and adjusted his Stetson. He didn't hurry but kept one eye on their surroundings and the other on Annie.

He watched as she slid the large door open enough so she could step inside. It was pitch-dark and from memory her hand found the switch, illuminating the interior. It was then she noticed Linc.

Her tone was sharp. "What are you doing, following me?"

"Wanted to make sure you didn't run into any of the local wildlife. There's been a mountain lion roaming around occasionally."

Her face blanched. "I didn't know." A soft nicker came from the end. Her face relaxed into a smile. "Do you think she knows I'm here?"

"You should go find out. Did you bring an apple?"

She patted her coat pocket and her eyes softened. "Of course."

He fell in step beside her and she paused to look in every stall, talking to each horse and asking questions about the new ones. Finally, she reached Bowie. Her head was hanging over the gate and Annie slid her arms around the mare's neck.

"Hey, girl. Did you miss me?"

Bowie nudged her side and tugged on her pocket. With a laugh she withdrew the apple and Bowie munched it down. Annie scratched the length of the mare's neck and she nickered. She shifted on her feet and Annie said, "Whoa. Look at her belly."

Linc leaned against the wall and stuck his hands in his jeans pockets. "I told you, she's got a big baby in there."

"Who is the sire?" She ran her hand down the length of Bowie's nose and talked softly so he almost couldn't hear the words. "You're a good girl and I've missed you."

He had missed her too but that wasn't something he'd share with anyone, let alone Annie.

"Butterscotch is the sire. He's over in Bozeman and Pops thought it would be a good strong bloodline for the future."

She nodded. "He had the best instincts when it came to breeding. Is Butterscotch a good-looking horse?"

"He's roughly sixteen hands and combined with Bowie's coloring and disposition, I have a lot of hope for the future."

She nodded and didn't speak, but she also didn't look at him. "I'd like to be here when she goes into labor."

"I'll make sure someone lets you know." It was awful they were talking like they were casual acquaintances. Could she feel the charge in the air? He could feel the intense pull to her, like two magnets being held apart when they should be together.

She kissed Bowie's nose. "I'll see you tomorrow and bring more apples. Okay, girl?" She started to walk the length of the barn and Linc again fell in step with her, matching her shorter stride.

"She looks good. Who's been looking after her?"

Should he confess and tell her he was taking

care of Bowie? "Zak Dawson manages this barn, but we all take turns looking after them."

"He's still here. Good to know." She gave him a side-eye. "Is he still seeing Allie Monroe?"

"No, they broke it off a while back and it's a subject we don't bring up."

She nodded. "A lot of that going on around here." Her steps slowed as they approached the main house. "Thanks for walking me up."

"Just part of the job. Making sure everything and everyone is safe."

"That's right; you're the ranch manager for the last, what, two years?"

"No, just about eighteen months."

She dropped her head and kicked the gravel. "It was easier for me to stay away knowing you were at Pops' side." She gave him a side-look. "I know it wasn't the right thing to do but yet it was." Her voice trailed off, absorbed into the comforting darkness.

"I know and I was happy to be here for him. He was a good man."

"Tough as rawhide though."

He saw a flash of her white teeth when she

smiled. For a moment it felt like old times except they weren't holding hands as they walked to the house after a date, both of them knowing Pops would be waiting in his office until she was safely inside.

She walked up the steps and paused at the top. "There's a black hole here."

He knew what she was talking about. The force of the ranch was gone and before he could censor his words, he asked, "Are you prepared to fill his boots?"

She perched on the railing and looked out into the darkness. "I'm not sure if I know how. He was driven to succeed and maybe if I hadn't left it would be different, but my time here was limited to summers and holidays. Living at boarding school and college kept me out of the day-to-day business."

"Annie, you're the smartest woman I've ever met." He held up a hand as she opened her mouth to protest. "I know you think I'm some sheltered ranch hand, but I know people and you've got his work ethic *and* his compassion for the people who work here."

"It's been a long day." She stood and brushed off the back of her jeans. "I'll see you tomorrow."

After the door softly closed behind her, Linc wondered what had just happened. One minute they were talking and the next she clammed up and disappeared into the safety of the house. He sank to the top step and leaned against the support post. The silence was comforting, but he needed to know if his Annie was still inside of the smart, polished businesswoman.

The front door banged and he glanced up. She was standing there with hands on hips, feet planted wide. He stood and she strode toward him, put her hands on his cool cheeks, and pulled him in, pressing her lips to his. The kiss was sweet and filled with volumes of unspoken words. She pulled away, looked him in the eyes, and her pretty blues didn't blink. She brushed her lips to his one more time and then withdrew and went back in the house.

Where her hands had touched his skin, the warmth lingered. Did this woman still have feelings for him or was that her way of getting closure on what had been between them? Whatever it was, he'd follow her wherever they were headed next. Tonight, he would fall asleep with the lingering smell of her sweet perfume and the taste of her kiss on his lips.

Chapter Three

Annie had a hard time falling asleep after kissing Linc. It was as if another woman had taken over her body and kissed him under the stars. It was a perfect night despite their history and her broken heart. She had never gotten over him. Every time she came back to the ranch, she hoped he'd search her out and say it was a mistake and she was the only woman he'd ever love. But that was a dream. All twisted up in the blankets, she kicked her legs free and flopped to her back.

Why did I kiss him? She punched the pillows. At this rate she wasn't going to get any sleep.

Giving up, she wandered into the kitchen in search of the cocoa and milk. She heated up a mug of milk in the microwave and stirred in a heaping spoonful of Mary's special cocoa mix.

The hall light clicked on. Mary was tying her bathrobe as she walked into the kitchen. "Can't sleep?"

She shook her head and handed Mary a mug of steaming cocoa before beginning to fix one for herself. "No. I'm keyed up."

Mary sat in one of the overstuffed chairs by the window and waited for Annie to join her. She pulled a throw out of the hassock and handed it to Annie.

"Thank you." Snuggled under the soft blanket, Annie sipped her cocoa and began to relax. "This is harder than I thought."

"Being here without Pops or seeing Linc?"

Mary always knew how to get right to the point.

"Both." She set her mug on the side table. "The house seems so empty, like a huge chasm in front of me and I don't know how to get to the other side."

Mary waited for her to continue.

"I kissed Linc tonight."

"Hmm, I didn't expect that for a few days."

That took her by surprise. "You thought we'd be playing kissy-face?"

"Not like just kissing to pass the time but there has always been something undeniable between the two of you. Time won't change that until you talk." She gave her brow a wiggle. "With real words, not raw emotions."

"It was a physical thing, just lips touching lips."

She clapped her hands together and gave a hoot. "You never said a word, just kissed him. And what propelled you to do that?"

"I don't know. I had just come inside and closed the door and a strong urge to turn around and see if his lips would feel as I remembered came over me."

"For the last fifteen years you've been thinking about how it would feel to kiss your first love and what did you find out?"

She looked at Mary. Her voice was hushed. "It all came rushing back."

"You're still in love with him, aren't you?"

With a half nod, she said, "I never stopped and I don't know what to do about it."

"Give it time and it will sort itself out. You'll see." Mary got up from the chair and placed a hand on her cheek. "I'll have breakfast ready at seven, but I'll keep it warm so you can sleep in."

"See you in the morning." Annie lingered in the chair while she finished her cocoa. The moon washed over the polished oak floor. Hours later she put the mugs in the sink and with a weight heavy on her heart, she went back to bed. This time she fell into a dreamless sleep.

Annie woke to the sound of a rooster crowing. She glanced at the clock and bolted out of bed and then ran to the slider. They had chickens now?

She rushed through getting ready, dressed in jeans, a lightweight cable-knit sweater, and tugged on her well-worn brown boots she had discovered in the back of her closet. It was like stepping into her skin, even if they had been stored in the closet for years. Somehow there wasn't a lick of dust on them. She knew that was Mary's handiwork. She loved this place as much as Annie did, and why wouldn't she? It was her home too and always would be.

She strode down the hall with purpose in her stride. Breakfast first, check on Bowie, and then tackle Pops' office, in that order. She followed the smell of coffee and what might just be her favorite muffins, and her stomach grumbled. Maybe there were some fresh eggs too.

She stopped short when she entered the kitchen. Gathered around the island was a bunch of ranch hands. Her smiled widened as one by one they gave her hearty hugs and welcomed her back.

Clint stepped forward and swept her off her feet. "Welcome home, shorty."

"That's Boss Shorty to you." She gave him a playful poke in the shoulder when he set her back down.

He tapped his forehead where his hat usually sat. "Ma'am."

She clutched her heart. "You're killing me, Clint. I'm not old enough to be called that."

"Annie, I'm pretty sure the unwritten rule is

once you hit the plus side of thirty-five, you're ma'am material."

He dropped a friendly kiss on her cheek. "There's a saddle waiting for my backside. Come find me when you have time to catch up."

"Will do."

The kitchen was cleared out of ranch hands, except for Linc and a tall gangly guy looking more like a late-blooming teenager rather than an adult. He stuck his hand out and gave her a guarded smile. "We haven't been formally introduced. I'm Rory Wilson and I've been handling office duties, sort of as a go-between for your grandfather and most of our suppliers." She watched his Adam's apple bob. "I'd like to show you some of the systems I've set up to see if you'd like me to change anything."

"Thanks, Rory. Can we do that in a few days? I want to go over what's in the office, and then I'll be ready to meet with you."

He gave her a broad smile. "Just let me know when. My office is in the dining hall."

"I would assume next to Quinn's kitchen?" She hoped her smile was reassuring. She didn't need anyone that Pops had hired quitting already. If Rory had lasted this long, he must be doing a solid job.

"That's the spot." He put his ball cap on and touched the brim. "Ma'am."

He strode out like he was on a mission. She caught Linc's amused smile directed at her.

"And what's up with you today?"

"I hope it was okay some of the guys came in to say hello. They're anxious to show you what they can do around here."

"I gathered that, but why the rush? Is anything happening I should know about?"

"Some of these men don't know you and vice versa. They're hoping nothing's gonna change here at Grace Star to affect their employment status."

She thought for a minute while pouring herself a cup of coffee. Mary was busy at the sink but hanging on every word. Annie held the pot out to Linc, and he extended his mug so she could refill it.

"Here's what you can pass along. If anyone stops pulling their weight one hundred percent, they have something to worry about. I expect everyone to do their jobs just as if Pops were still alive. I may be a new face to some, but I'm Pops' granddaughter and in my blood, I'm a rancher too."

"Does this mean you won't be selling the ranch?"

Now that surprised her. What would make Linc even think that was a realistic option? After she analyzed the numbers, if profits weren't steady, she'd be ruthless and cut the fat. It was something she knew how to do—turn a business profitable, even if that meant selling it. But in this case, that would be the very last resort after she exhausted all ways to save her home. "Why would you ask that?"

He slowly sipped the hot coffee while looking at her over the rim. It seemed as if he was trying to decide what to say.

"Stop stalling, Linc. If you have something on your mind, out with it."

"Sometime last October, Pops said there was an offer to buy the ranch. Wanted to turn it into a fancy resort. He didn't want to sell, basically told the guy who approached him that as long as he drew breath, this would remain a working ranch."

"He never told me." She sagged against the counter. Did that mean the ranch was in financial trouble?

"I'm gonna bet there were a lot of things you didn't know about the ranch, but you can learn. There's plenty of time."

She gave a curt nod. "I appreciate you filling me in." She lifted her eyes to meet his. The electricity from his searing look zapped her heart. It would be easy to cross the small space between them and fall into his arms, but the moment of insanity from last night was not going to be repeated anytime soon or at all. She had a job to do and kissing her former love was not on the to-do list.

"Earth to Annie."

She realized he had been talking and she felt heat flush her cheeks. "I'm sorry. I lost my train of thought for a minute."

A slow and sexy grin slid from one side of his mouth to the other. "Care to share?"

She shook her head. "It's personal."

He dropped his voice. "Yes, it was very personal."

Damn, he knew she was thinking about the kiss. Well, she needed to stop. Linc worked for her now, and business and pleasure didn't mix. She jammed her hand in her front jeans pocket.

"Are we still on for one?" A safe subject like their meeting was much easier to handle.

Mary cleared her throat. "I was going to fix some beef barley soup for lunch. Linc, why don't you come up around noon and have lunch with Annie. I'll be running out and there'll be more than enough for two."

Annie snapped her head around and Mary gave her an innocent smile.

He placed his mug in the sink as if he'd been doing this all their lives and leaned in. Was he going to kiss her?

With his lips close to her ear, he said, "I'll be up at noon if that suits?"

She didn't want to look like a jerk or that she couldn't be in the same room with him, sharing a meal. Besides, it wasn't a date. It could be a working lunch; that was the ticket.

Giving them both a bright smile, she said, "Excellent idea, a working lunch. That will give us more time to talk about the ranch, spring planting, and an entire list of other topics that I need to catch up on."

He never blinked or let on that lunch was just lunch. "See you at noon then." He gave Mary a kiss on the cheek. "Any chance you might make some of your famous biscuits to go with it?"

Annie could see the twinkle in his eyes.

Mary patted his cheek. Like Annie, she had always treated Linc like he was one of her own kids. "I think I can manage that."

After the back door closed with a soft *thud*, Annie sank down at the kitchen table. Her knees had been knocking from being so close to Linc. This was going to be harder than she had originally thought. The more time she spent with him, the bigger the reminder she never got over him.

"Mary?"

"Yes, child." Her eyes sparkled with mischief. "Are you ready for breakfast?" She took oven mitts and pulled two plates from the oven and removed the foil coverings. "I hope you're hungry. I made huckleberry pancakes and sausage."

She kept herself moving, setting the plates on the table and then placing a small bowl of fruit, some syrup, and orange juice glasses on the table.

"Mary, this looks delicious, but why did you ask Linc to have lunch with me?"

She took her seat across from Annie. "Pops and Linc often had lunch together and talked about what was going on. I know you have a list of questions a mile long in your head and I find it's best to talk over a shared meal." She gave a nonchalant one-shoulder shrug. "No ulterior motive."

She clapped her hands together. "Ah-ha! I knew it. Are you trying to play matchmaker?"

She held the pitcher of syrup poised to pour and placed her other hand over her heart. Trying to feign shock, she said, "Who me? I'm merely doing for you what I did for Pops. Nothing more, nothing less."

Annie took the pitcher from Mary and proceeded to drown her pancakes in syrup. Her stomach grumbled in anticipation. "Just do me one favor; don't get any ideas." Very unladylike, she filled her mouth with pancakes and rolled her eyes back in her head. Mumbling, she said, "Now this is what pancakes should taste like."

Once their plates were empty and Annie was stuffed, they chatted about the vegetable garden Mary had planned for this year. Annie was worried about Mary working so hard and offered to lend a hand when it was needed.

"Now, don't go worrying. You've got enough to think about. Besides, two years ago, Pops had the boys build me raised beds for all my garden areas so I don't even need to kneel on the ground."

"Do we have enough to grow all that we need to can and freeze?" Annie knew the value of having a supply of food on hand. Even in this modern era it was important due to storms that could whip up, leaving them cut off from town. Plus, it was more cost-effective feeding the ranch hands from what they could grow.

"We don't garden like we used to. We're buying more food in bulk and filling the freezers that way. I just can't spend the entire day outside anymore. The sun gives me headaches now."

She didn't like the sound of that. Was Mary ill?

She patted Annie's hand and gave it a reassuring squeeze. "I see that look on your face and I'm fine, just slowing down a bit."

"What if we hired someone to help garden? It would be their job from getting a larger garden ready through harvest and preserving. It might be more cost-effective and certainly better quality of food for our employees."

Mary's eyes lit up. Gardening had always been her passion. "I'd love to have the extra hands."

"I'll talk to Quinn and see what he thinks the needs are. We can use whatever acreage is needed to grow vegetables for the ranch. I'd like us to be providing the very best for everyone and not just us."

"You've got a good heart, Annie."

"Well, it just makes sense. Good nutrition equals healthy people. It's a win for us all."

"I can talk to Quinn about what vegetables are a must-have for his kitchen if you'd like."

"Mary, I'm counting on you to oversee the project, work with Quinn and whoever we hire to take care of the gardens. Is The Trading Post still open?"

She nodded. "Yes, and I'm sure if I place an order, they can get us everything we need. But I'll need to get started."

Annie nodded. "Good and I'll ask Linc about where we might find a gardener. Maybe one of the ranch hands has a green thumb."

"Be sure to add that to your list of questions for Linc."

Annie laughed. "Stop pushing, Mary."

Chapter Four

Linc checked his watch. He had enough time to walk over to the main house with ten minutes to spare before his meeting with Annie. Mary was quite the character, arranging lunch so he and Annie could spend even more time together. It was good someone around here still believed in love.

On the way out of his office he picked his hat up off the cabinet and checked to make sure his shirt was tucked in. Not that Annie would care if he was wearing a tee shirt or a suit; at least she hadn't when they were younger. But he could see she'd changed. She wasn't the same carefree girl from years ago. Heck, he wasn't the same guy either.

He tapped on the kitchen door and walked in, setting his hat upside down on the small table near the back door. He took a seat at the island, then hesitated. Maybe he needed to wait until someone answered the door. Mary was slipping her coat on and gave him a warm smile.

"She's in Pops' office. Go on down and when you're ready, the soup is simmering on the stove and fresh biscuits are in the basket next to it."

He kissed her cheek. "Everything smells great."

She patted his arm. "If your sweet tooth kicks in, I made your favorite, oatmeal scotchies, and they're in the cookie jar."

"Did you happen to remember they're also Annie's favorites too?"

A gleam came into her eye. "Go. Find her. But be patient with her. Coming home has been harder than she thought it would be."

Once again Linc's protective streak wanted to stand between her and all the hurts of the world, but he knew all he could do was stand by her side and wait for her to ask for help.

He tapped on the doorjamb and pushed it open. "Hey, Annie."

She gave him a half-hearted smile. "Come on in. I'm going through a stack of invoices. Some of them are overdue."

He took a seat in the old wooden chair across from her and stretched his legs out in front of him, crossing his boots at his ankles.

She raised a brow. "Comfy?"

"I am. Thanks." He gave her a smile, trying to tamp down the tension that surrounded her. It was easy to see when she gave in as her shoulders were less rigid. "Tell me what's going on. How late are the invoices?"

"Two months. Any idea why?"

"Pops didn't spend much time in the office the last couple of months and no one could sign checks."

She tipped her head to one side. "When I was home at Christmas, he had me stop in and see Cora at the bank and become a signature for all the accounts." She frowned. "I wish someone had said something when I was here for the funeral. I would have taken care of things then. I'd hate for our suppliers to think we're having financial troubles."

"Rory reached out and explained what happened. Pops had been a steady customer for years, so they were happy to wait until you got here."

"I'll have to get those checks out this afternoon and get things back on track."

She pushed back from the desk and stretched her arms over her head. Her rising shirt gave him a glance of a small sliver of skin. His mouth went dry and his mind flashed back to when they'd spend hours lying next to the river on a warm summer day, kissing, his hand on her warm skin, but they had never moved beyond that. He had wanted them to wait, but then it was too late. She was gone.

"I'm starving. Did Mary leave yet?"

He pushed all thoughts of them riverside to the back of his mind. "I met her while she was on her way out when I came in and lunch is all set. All we have to do is dish it up."

She held out her hand just like she used to and

color flushed her cheeks and she withdrew it. "We should eat on the patio. I've spent all morning inside."

He rose from the chair. "Good to know that hasn't changed."

She gave him a sharp look. "What do you mean by that?"

He held up his hands in surrender. "Nothing. We were always happiest when we were outside and not cooped up; that's all."

He trailed behind her as she marched down the hall. He'd better think before he spoke again. She was like getting caught up in stinging nettles, but nothing he couldn't deal with.

They moved around the kitchen like a well-practiced team. He got the bowls from the cabinets, and she ladled up the soup. She added the overfull bowls to the tray with the basket of biscuits, and Linc filled two glasses with water.

"If the soup tastes as good as it smells, Mary will have outdone herself as usual." He took the tray from her hand. "You get the door."

She opened her mouth and then closed it. If she wanted to argue about carrying the tray, she changed her mind. He didn't want everything to be an argument between them. Working together was the only way to keep the ranch running smoothly.

They ate in companionable silence. For some it would have seemed awkward, but Linc guessed being at the ranch was working its magic. It was like old times seeing Annie watch the birds frolicking in the birdbath in the flower garden as Mary's kitty skulked across the grass on the hunt. The sounds of cattle softly lowing was as soothing for him as it had always been for her too.

"Rumor has it your favorite cookie is in the jar."

Her brow arched. "And you had us come out without them?"

He chuckled and stacked the dirty dishes on the tray. "I'll get us a couple. You relax."

She leaned back in the chair and closed her eyes. "Make it three a piece."

He placed the dishes in the sink and took the jar of cookies to the patio along with a pitcher of milk. It was the only combination as far as he was concerned, and to get through the next part of the day, they might need the entire jar.

He held the canister of cookies for Annie while she drained her water before reaching for the pitcher of milk and filling her glass. "You always have the best ideas." She tapped her glass to his. "Let's drink to our first successful business meeting."

He kept his eyes locked on hers. "Do you remember the first time we sat here drinking milk and eating cookies?"

She averted her eyes. "I was fourteen and you were sixteen. My parents had passed away and it was the first summer I lived with Pops full-time."

He nodded. "You put on a brave face for him but when it was just us sitting out here, you'd talk about your mom and dad."

"I didn't have to worry about him overhearing me and making him sad." She dunked a cookie in the milk. "And I never wanted him to think I was angry with him for moving me here."

"He knew how hard it was for you. After all, he lost his son and daughter-in-law. You were both hurting."

She nibbled on the cookie. "We never really talked about them except at holidays, but in the normal course of our time together, we just didn't. It's easier to understand now that I'm older. Mary was amazing during those first few weeks. Every time she came into my room, she'd find me crying and she'd hold me until I didn't have any tears left. She's always been my bonus grandmother."

"Mine too."

She wiped her mouth with a napkin. "We need to skip the trip down memory lane and deal with the present."

He knew focusing on facts was her salvation and shield. There would be another time they could talk about the past. He let her take the lead on what she wanted to discuss.

"This morning Mary and I were talking about increasing the size of our vegetable garden. I plan on talking with Quinn to see what he thinks we'd need to harvest to offset the expense to feed us all for the winter."

"That's ambitious." He leaned forward and tented his hands. "How much land do you think we'll need to allocate? I'm sure I could free up a ranch hand to help out."

"That would be helpful to prep the land, but I intend on hiring someone to work the gardens, and if it goes well, next year we'll add a greenhouse too. I want Grace Star to be a sustainable property. I heard a rooster crowing this morning; how many chickens do we have?"

"Quinn's keeping about twelve, I think. He uses the eggs to supplement what he purchases."

She said, "Hold that thought. I'll be right back."

She hurried into the house and a few minutes later she was back with a laptop. "I need to start a list." She tapped a few keys and said, "How many full-time employees do we have right now?"

"It's been bouncing a bit, forty to forty-five and we'll bring in extra help if we need it for haying."

"Does that include everyone on the property, including me and Mary?"

"Let's use a round number of fifty."

She tapped on her keys and looked up. "I'll talk to Quinn about the long-term needs. Do you have any ideas for an experienced gardener looking for work who might want to join us? They have to be willing to build this from the ground up. I like giving people an opportunity, but I need someone who understands how to grow vegetables since our season is short, which is why I'm already thinking about a greenhouse to extend the growing season."

"You're serious about this?" There was one thing about Annie he admired; when she wanted to do something, she committed herself to a project. If she wanted to plow up an acre or two to feed everyone, then he'd do all he could for her to be successful.

"Very. But I know we're kind of late to the party this year. I'd like to hire someone pretty quickly and get seeds in the ground. Oh, and I'm going to have Mary supervise since she is our resident garden expert."

"That's a good idea, but this person will have to work with Quinn too. Since I'm assuming there should be enough produce to can during harvest, that means he'll need access to the kitchen and you know how Quinn feels about his kitchen."

She grinned. "A smidge overprotective."

"I'll make a few calls this afternoon and see if I can get names for you."

"Excellent." She concentrated on her screen again and then asked, "Do you have anything specific you'd like to address before I run down my list?"

He wanted to talk about what happened last night on the front porch but wasn't sure if that was on her list. He shook his head. "You go first and if there's something that you didn't cover, I'll let you know."

For the next couple of hours, they talked non-stop. Annie was catching up on the business and asked thoughtful questions about each employee. She seemed pleased with all his answers.

"Now tell me, do you think that resort investor is still poking around?"

"I haven't seen him and Pops made it quite clear the spread was staying a working ranch."

She tapped her short, polished nail on the glass tabletop. "I've been thinking about that. If someone came poking around, there might be an income stream we've overlooked."

His heart sank. Was this where she was about to tell him she'd consider selling for the right price?

"This wouldn't be the cheapest ranch to purchase in Montana so why were they interested? My guess," she continued before he could respond to her question. "It's the river. The trout fishing is some of the best in the state, and coupled with the beauty of the ranch, it does have eye appeal. But if someone wanted to invest, I think we should consider opening the ranch up as a working resort."

"You want to become a pleasure dude ranch?" He tried, but couldn't hold back the sneer.

She laughed loudly. "I think that needs to be rephrased, but in a manner of speaking."

She held up her hand as he felt his neck and face get hot. She was going to be a sellout after all. How could she do that after all Pops had done to protect it?

"Now don't go getting your stirrups rusted. What I'm saying is we've got a lot of land around here and I might want to take a small area, put up fancy cabins, less than ten, and give people the real ranch experience."

He pushed back from the table. "That is not what Pops would have wanted you to do." He made sure each word was enunciated just to make his point.

She gave him a long look. "I've spent the morning looking over the numbers, and obviously I've just scratched the surface, but if we want to thrive long term and not just scrape by, we have to look at all options."

"We've been doing just fine."

Her eyes narrowed. "When did you become a business analyst?"

"You don't have to have some fancy degree and work for a high-powered firm to know that one plus one equals two and subtract one for expenses, it still leaves you with a dollar profit."

"I never said it wasn't profitable, but I'm not going to be content to let this ranch wither and die on the side of the trail because I refuse to look at all the information with a keen eye."

"Isn't that what Pops has been doing for years?"

"No, he's been running the ranch the same way for the last fifty years. New generation, new ideas."

"Don't go changing things that work, Annie."

She stood up and straightened her shoulders. "Is your last name Grace?"

He knew where she was going with this. He was the hired help, and she was the owner. All decisions, no matter what he might think, were ultimately hers.

"And if you don't explore this new idea of yours, does it mean you're gonna sell and then hightail it back to Boston?"

"I don't intend to spend sleepless nights worrying about if I'm gonna make payroll."

"Are things that bad?" His stomach clenched. Pops should have told him times were tough.

"Not now. But I won't let it get that bad either." She gave him a serious glare. "I need to know you've got my back with all my decisions. If I can't trust you, this relationship won't work."

There was that word. Relationship. He didn't want Annie to wonder where his loyalty lay.

"I'd do anything for you, Annie. Never doubt

that I've got your back and I'm your go-to man. I won't let you down."

Her face softened but remained serious at the same time. "I appreciate that, Linc." She stuck her hand out to him. "Partners?"

He took her small, soft hand in his calloused one. He'd like to be partners in every way possible. *Slow down, cowboy. She's been home for twenty-four hours.* Annie knew a handshake was his bond. It was his way, the only way.

Chapter Five

A week later Annie was slouched on the front porch in the swing, drinking coffee and thinking about Linc. She knew his handshake was his bond to her. He'd back all her decisions in public even if they'd fight like mountain lions behind closed doors. Too bad he had only been willing to give her a promise about business.

At least things were progressing. After talking with Quinn regarding the vegetable garden and given the late start, he suggested they concentrate on cooler weather crops—cabbage, lettuces, potatoes, and other root vegetables that will still continue to grow and produce into late fall. Mary was planning tomatoes for her raised bed garden so that was a plus. In fact, her mouth watered just imagining plucking a grape tomato from the vine and popping it in her mouth, bursting with sweet warm juice from the sun.

Despite the early hour, ranch hands were already busy for the day. Life was never quiet or dull —well, maybe except for winter when a snowstorm hit. Today she'd go down and check on Bowie to see how the momma was coming along. Maybe she'd even run into Linc while she was in the barn. But her first task was putting an ad online for the gardener since Linc hadn't mentioned anyone yet. She needed to get someone in place like yesterday.

She noticed Linc's truck coming in the direction of the house. He must be going to the back fields since past the house was the most direct route. She sat up a little straighter in the swing when he pulled up in front of the porch and rolled the window down and leaned out.

"Morning, Annie." His grin was wide and she'd guess his eyes were twinkling behind his sunglasses.

She was pleased to see he was finally wearing them. "Good morning. What brings you by this sunny morning?" She crossed to the railing and perched on it.

"I was headed into town and thought you might want to tag along. I'm going to the hardware store and there's a bulletin board where people advertise to work around the area, you know like gardeners." He took his sunglasses off and propped them on the dash.

"I was going to put an ad online."

"Annie, that's the way people do stuff in other places, but here in River Junction, you know the best way to find good help is the personal touch. You know Jeremy Taylor, right?"

She nodded.

"Well, he still owns the place and he knows everyone personally who tacks up a sign. It's almost like he's done the interviewing for you."

That did hold a certain appeal. She could quiz him on anyone that might look like they had potential. She glanced down at her bare feet, gray yoga pants, and Life is Good tee shirt.

"I'm not fit to go anywhere. But after I get dressed, I'll head in and my first stop will be to chat with Jeremy."

He pushed open the pickup's door and stepped out. He looked handsome in his tight-fitting jeans, scuffed cowboy boots, and chambray button-down shirt. Her fingers tingled as she wanted to run them through his dark hair to see if the strands of silver were as soft as she imagined.

"I'll wait. Go get dressed. I'll just grab a coffee and see if Mary has any cookies left."

He took the porch steps two at a time and dipped his head to her. With a saucy smile, he said, "Time's a-waistin'. Put a wiggle on it."

It was a shock to realize she had wanted him to kiss her. She turned her head so he wouldn't see the flush of her cheeks. "I'll be ready in ten."

He chuckled and held open the screen door. "I'll give you fifteen."

She walked in and looked at him over her shoulder. "Is that a challenge I hear?"

He lifted a shoulder and said, "Only if you

want to make it one." He pointed to the back of the house. "I'll be in the kitchen."

Before she could walk away, he gave her a playful swat on her bum which wasn't what she had expected again. Today was going to be interesting and not as dull as sitting in front of a computer screen.

"Twelve minutes was impressive." Linc glanced at her from behind the wheel. She had offered to drive but only to see what he'd say. She was happy to ride shotgun.

"It would have been ten but since you graciously gave me fifteen, I split the difference."

His gaze ran over her. "Nice jeans. Did you get those in Boston?"

She ran a hand over her deep-blue jeans, and yes, they happened to be new. "No, online. I wasn't sure how many pairs I had here, so I ordered a few new things and had them shipped here." She was pleased he seemed to notice the small details.

"And?"

She gave him a curious look. "Oh, you're wondering what I found in my closet when I got back?"

He laughed. "Well, it seems like there's more to the story than you just went shopping."

"I've got enough jeans to last me the rest of my life—and tees too. I'll need some warmer clothes for winter, but I've got time."

"So does that mean you're staying?"

"I don't have plans to return to Boston, at least not now. I'm committed to learning all I can about the ranch and there's more improvements I'm looking to make."

His words were slow and measured. "Nothing has to be done overnight, you know."

She wanted to ask him about that last night they were together, the night he broke her heart, but it was best it remained left unsaid.

"When is the vet coming to check on Bowie? I'm getting concerned she hasn't had her foal yet." She adjusted the shoulder strap on her seat belt as she felt the frown cross her face. "You don't think anything's wrong, do you?"

"The foal is moving around and other than

being huge, she seems to be tolerating the pregnancy okay." He touched her leg and returned his hand to the steering wheel. "I know how important she is to you. I promise I'll do all I can to make sure she and her foal are healthy."

She liked how it felt to have even the slightest touch from him. Instead of her face betraying her innermost thoughts, she looked out at the passing landscape. There was no place like this on earth. Home. It was too bad she didn't have anyone to share her life with. Linc didn't want that and the guys she had dated back East wouldn't have wanted to live here. Heck, they hadn't even wanted to visit for longer than a weekend which was why she never brought any man home to meet her grandfather.

"I remember it was my sixteenth birthday and when most kids were getting cars, Pops gave me a yearling. He was so excited when Buck got her out of the trailer. I'll never forget that moment. We were standing near the barn. She was the most beautiful horse I had ever seen, her gold coat in sharp contrast to her white mane and tail. From the moment I placed my hand on her soft nose, I was hooked."

"I'll bet she was too. I wish I'd been there to see that. That was the summer I started working on the ranch and I was learning how to repair fencing."

"As soon as you got here, you came to the barn. I was walking her around the paddock."

"Pops told me to find you when I got done for the day. You made quite the pair, with the contrast of your dark hair and her golden coat. Yin and yang."

She gave him a sharp look. "You know, I never did thank you for taking care of her when I was at school."

"She's a great horse and I wouldn't let just anyone take care of her."

And that's when it dawned on her. "You've been doing that all these years, haven't you?"

He kept his eyes on the two-lane road in front of him. "Guilty."

"Why?" Her heart slowed. Would he say something sweet or that it was just part of the job working on the ranch and taking care of all the animals.

"I just did."

His voice was gruff, and the tone indicated the subject was closed. At least for now. She'd circle back to it another time. She grew quiet and enjoyed the rest of the ride.

As they approached the small town of River Junction, he said, "After we hit the hardware store, we can take a walk down Main Street and you can see what's changed. After all, we can spare twenty minutes and walk from one end to the other."

"It's nice to see some things haven't changed." She grinned. "Mary said they've added a few more shops to attract tourists so it might take twenty-five and if we get lucky, we both might discover new stores."

With a snort Linc slowed the truck and parked in front of a weathered wooden building with a big wooden sign in bold red letters that said, The Trading Post, which was much more than a hardware store. It was also the feed store, work clothes and boots, garden center, and fish and game store. It was the perfect answer to an all-purpose store in the west.

He turned the engine off and grinned. "The big shopper that I am, if I need something, this is the spot."

She gave him a playful punch in the shoulder. "Then it's a good thing Jeremy keeps his doors open."

He faked a shudder. "Can you imagine if he went out of business? The rest of the town wouldn't know what to do." He pushed open his door. "Coming?"

They entered the store with its gray concrete floor and endless rows of well-stocked shelves. Every time Linc walked in, he'd swear the store expanded, but really Jeremy rotated the stock based on the seasons, putting what was most likely needed near the front.

Annie paused to look at the ball caps on display and moved on to tees with funny ranch slogans, all good for any tourist who might wander in. She got why he'd have stuff like this on hand to appeal to folks with cash to spend. "It hasn't really changed, has it?"

Linc said, "It's been like this since I was a kid."

Linc's family weren't ranchers; they ran Coop's gas station on the corner of town. Mr. Cooper thought he was clever when he named his business almost forty years ago.

"Is that Annie Grace in my store?"

She could feel her smile widen as Jeremy opened his arms.

"Come 'ere, kid, and give this old guy a hug. It's been a while."

The smile faded from his face since they all knew it had only been a couple of months since the last time he saw her, at Pops' funeral.

She flew across the store and wrapped her arms around the older man as he lifted her off her feet. He'd been a good friend of Pops.

"Jeremy, it's so good to see you." She held him tight and when he set her on the floor, she was still smiling.

"How long have you been back?"

"A little over a week." She tugged the hem of

her tee back into place and brushed her hair off her cheeks. "I've been getting settled and catching up with what's happening, but I'll be honest. I'm on a mission today."

"When are you not?" He gave her an indulgent smile. "But how can I help?"

"I want to plant a vegetable garden."

He chuckled and shook his head. "I think Mary might have something to say about that; she's already got things growing, I'm sure."

"This isn't to interfere with Mary's, but I want to have a huge garden to feed my ranch hands. I've been talking to Quinn about what we'll need, and I know we're getting a late start since we haven't even tilled up a space yet and worked the soil but there's still stuff we can grow."

"I can set you up with whatever you need." He moved to grab a cart.

"Well, seeds and stuff are only part of what I need."

"Oh?" he drawled. "What's more important than supplies?"

She looked at Linc and then Jeremy. "I'm

looking to hire someone who has the knowledge to grow food in our slice of paradise. For right now, it'd be part time but next year, if this goes well, I'd want to expand it to a full-time position." She jabbed her thumb in Linc's direction. "He said you still have a board where people post, looking for jobs and such."

He rubbed his hand over his chin, and after a moment, his face lit up. "I can do you one better." He walked to the back of the store, his steps steady but with a bounce too.

Linc looked at Annie as they could hear him talking to someone, and now she was curious. It didn't take long before Jeremy came back to the front of the store.

"Polly, this is Annie Carson. She owns Grace Star Ranch out on Red Mountain Road."

Annie took a step toward the tall, slender girl and shook her hand. "It's nice to meet you."

"Likewise." Polly glanced at Linc and gave him a smile. "Hey, Linc."

He smiled hello and gestured to the patch on her shirt. "I didn't know you were working here. I thought you left town."

"I guess River Junction kind of grew on me and I came back a couple of months ago. There wasn't much available so I picked up odd jobs, gardening, cleaning a few stores in town and the like, but I'm here two days a week."

"Polly, would you have an interest working part-time for me out at the ranch?" Annie gave her an encouraging smile.

Confusion flitted over her face and her words were slow. "I'm not looking to be a ranch hand."

With a laugh, Annie said, "I'm looking for someone who wants to grow vegetables for my employees. Work with Quinn, our cook, and Mary who runs all of us. Longer term, if this season goes well, I plan on building a greenhouse too so this position would become full time."

Her eyes grew round. "You're looking for a gardener to grow vegetables to feed everyone who works for you?"

"That's the plan." Annie beamed.

Linc could see the two women would get along since they were both passionate about the future.

Polly took a step back. "Wow. Do you have a plot ready to plant?"

"I will when I hire the right person. I firmly believe to be successful I need to buy in from the beginning. So, do you want to come out and see the ranch? If you're interested, you can have a say in where I'm thinking about plowing up an acre or two."

Polly's face paled. "I don't know if we can get a good harvest this year if the soil hasn't been prepped and I'd hate to let you down."

"Come out and take a look. Talk to Mary and I'll introduce you to Quinn. If you want to take the job for the season, with next year pending, I'll take it."

She looked at Jeremy and Linc. "But," she stammered, "you don't know me."

Annie nodded. "True, and you don't know me, but what do you say? Are you interested in seeing what I have in mind?"

With a laugh, Polly said, "How's seven tomorrow?"

"How about eight? I need coffee if you want me to be coherent."

Linc nodded with a grin, seemingly pleased with this outcome. It was obvious Polly needed the job and Annie liked to surround herself with people who wanted to work. Hopefully this was a huge plus in her win column.

Chapter Six

Annie and Linc strolled down Main Street. She took in the small shops and when they got to the end of their stroll, she checked the time. "Twenty-seven minutes."

Linc threw back his head and laughed. It was a rich, heart-skipping sound. "Leave it to you to time our walk."

"Well, I wanted to see how much the town grew. It's a good indication that people are doing well."

He tipped his hat back so it was now perched on the crown of his head. "Interesting way to look at it but you always did have the best way to view life, through indicators of progress."

"Which leads to success." She jumped when the firehouse whistle blew just like it had every day at noon. "Hungry?"

"Startle you?" His eyes crinkled when he grinned. "And have you ever met a cowboy that wasn't?"

She ignored his question. "Let's head over to the diner and I'll buy lunch." This way he wouldn't think of it, even remotely, as a date. She looked away. *So why did that even pop in my head?*

"Tell you what. We can each buy our own meals so there is no confusion, since I might misconstrue your intentions by paying for my meal." He gave her a saucy wink.

Now she had to chuckle. "Good point."

Filler Up Diner was midway down Main Street, closer to the hardware store. Both businesses had been long standing in the community and always family run. Annie liked the stability this town gave her. Her parents died in the plane crash in the Rocky Mountains right after she turned thirteen. Living here had been the balm to her soul. Pippa wanted her to have the best education and convinced Pops she should go to a good boarding school for girls. As much as Pippa loved Montana, she wanted her only granddaughter to have choices on what her future might be. So, all holidays and summers had been much sweeter since every time she came home, there was a time limit. Was this time going to be different? Would she finally put down roots instead of wondering what came next in life?

Linc held the glass and metal door open for her. She said thanks and stepped inside, greeted by the tantalizing aroma of food cooking making her stomach grumble. The diner hadn't changed a bit. It had the same black and white tiles on the floor; booths with bright-blue vinyl cushions lined the front windows; tables were packed in close, and it still had the counter with short stools in the very front with the mirror so people at the counter could watch what was going on behind them.

"Would you look at who's here? It's Annie and Linc. Why, I haven't seen the two of you together in years." Maggie Brady grabbed two vinyl-coated menus and came around the counter. She pulled Annie into a bear hug. "It's been too long, Annie. But it's good to have you home."

"Thanks, Maggie." When they were all in high school, they used to hang out together like teenagers did, getting into minor mischief but basically just swimming, horseback riding, and letting off steam once they all got their chores done.

"How long ya here for?"

Annie glanced at Linc, not like he knew the answer either. "I'm not sure. It's open-ended."

"If ya want my vote, I'd love to have you stay put. I've missed you." She hugged her again and, in her ear, softly said, "I'm real sorry again about Pops. He was a great guy."

"Thanks for coming to the funeral. I didn't get a chance to talk to everyone. I never expected so many people stopping at the house after the cemetery." It was good she could talk about the funeral without crying for a change. But this wasn't that kind of conversation, just two old friends catching up a bit.

"Pops never met anyone he didn't call friend." She ushered Annie and Linc to a booth. "Have a seat and I'll be back in a minute for your order. Do you want coffee?"

Annie perked up. "Do you still have your mom's famous lemonade?"

She beamed when Annie mentioned it. "We sure do. Two glasses?"

Linc nodded. "Of course."

Annie looked at the menu, but she knew what she was having. She'd never had light and fluffy pancakes like they served here and she sure as heck couldn't make them.

Linc set his menu aside. "Let me guess. Pancakes, crispy bacon, and a few scrambled eggs."

She tipped her head to the side. "Am I that predictable?"

"No, we've just spent a lot of time together." He leaned forward. "I've missed that. And you."

Her mouth went dry and Maggie's timing was impeccable as she set down two large glasses of lemonade.

"Linc, your usual? Fried eggs, bacon, toast, and muffin of the day?"

He nodded. Maggie didn't write anything down.

"Annie, let me guess. The pancake special?"

Annie laughed. "Thanks, Maggie."

The diner began to fill up with tourists and locals alike and soon Maggie was busy. A teenage girl came out of the back who looked like a younger version of her old friend. The girl walked past their table and said hello.

"Is that Maggie's daughter?"

Linc said, "Yup, she's the spitting image of her mom, isn't she? Suzie's dad ran out on them when she was just a little girl. It's been the two of them ever since."

"I had no idea. That had to have been hard, raising a daughter and working at the diner. I know the hours they're open and it's way before the rooster crows."

"She owns the diner now. Her parents decided to retire and they're living in Arizona. But she's done a great job raising Suzie."

She put a straw in her cup and took a long drink. Sweet and tart and ice-cold, just like she remembered. "When we were walking around town, I was thinking how nothing has really changed here, but that's only on the surface.

People grew up, started families, suffered sorrows, and kept going."

Linc looked at her for several moments and she couldn't figure out what he was thinking. Finally, he said, "It's called life, Annie."

On the way back to the ranch, Linc was quiet. A few times Annie caught him glancing her way. Had lunch not agreed with him? She knew her belly was comfortably full, but she couldn't eat like that at every meal and see the numbers on the scale stay the same. After all, she wasn't a teenager anymore.

Tired of the silence, she blurted out, "Why did you break up with me by telling me you wanted to date other girls?"

The truck slowed. Linc gave no other indication he heard her, but his jaw twitched. She had struck a nerve. They drove for a couple more miles, then pulled off and parked under a small tree.

His voice was steady and he looked straight ahead. "We were headed down different paths. I could see you were going to have an amazing future after you graduated college. Coming back to River Junction because of me would have limited what you could experience. I didn't want you to sacrifice your future."

"What are you talking about? You could have gone wherever I was; you didn't have to stay here."

He gave her a hard look. "I know who I am, a man working the land in Montana. I never wanted to do anything else. You're smart, ambitious, and you needed to discover who you were meant to be too."

"Instead of having a discussion with me, you just took matters into your own hands and broke my heart." She folded her arms across her chest and looked out the side window. "Was there a girl waiting in the wings you wanted to date?"

"Does it matter?"

She snapped her head around. "It matters to me, so yes. I have a right to know."

He hung his head. "Over the last fifteen years, I haven't dated much."

What did that mean, that he had dated someone after she left or that he hadn't?

"No one serious?"

"It doesn't matter, Annie. I like my life as it is, simple and uncomplicated." He put the truck in drive and pulled back onto the road, gravel kicking up from the tires in their wake.

But Linc hadn't asked her about her dating life. Did he want to know? This conversation left her with more questions, not less. She studied his profile. He was more handsome today than he had been all those years ago. Her heart ached. He had made decisions for both of them. In her gut, she knew they had been drifting through their adult lives, never really connecting to another, at least not like the bond they'd shared. It didn't matter if she didn't want to acknowledge it out loud; she had always loved Lincoln Cooper. He had gotten under her skin when she was a teenager and that's where he stayed.

When they got back to the ranch, he stopped at the main house.

"Thanks for taking me into town today. I'm glad I met Polly and got that project going."

"Not a problem." His voice was gruff.

"I'm going to check on Bowie in a while. Will you be around?"

He gave a curt nod and said, "If you can't find me, just use the walkie."

She closed the truck door and he turned out of the driveway in the direction of the manager's cabin. *Well, that conversation made things uncomfortable.*

Time to find Mary and give her the good news about Polly, and maybe she could whip up some muffins for coffee in the morning after they walked the grounds to pick the new garden spot.

Later in the afternoon Annie finally put on her barn boots. Linc's voice came over the walkie.

"Annie, are you there?"

"I'm here."

"Come on down to the barn. Bowie's in labor and she's hit stage two and it won't be long until we meet our baby."

"On my way." She yelled the good news to Mary and without waiting for acknowledgement, she took off running to the horse barn. This was something she was not going to miss.

She skidded at the entrance door and jogged to Bowie's stall at the end of the barn. Linc and a woman whom she presumed was the vet were leaning against the stall, just watching. This wasn't Bowie's first foal, but anything could go wrong so it was prudent to be cautious.

He turned and grinned. "We haven't seen the front hooves yet, but I expect to any moment now." He pulled Annie close, his arm loose around her shoulders. "Are you excited?"

She nodded. "And worried about my girl. I've heard having babies is tough stuff."

"This is Allison Howard, our vet."

"It's nice to meet you." Annie shook her hand. "I'm Annie Grace and Bowie is my pride and joy."

Annie put Allison at roughly fifty. Her short, no-nonsense steely-gray hair and the lines around her eyes and mouth spoke of a woman who smiled often.

"Pleasure to meet you, Annie. I don't think you have much to worry about with Bowie. She's in excellent health and I've been monitoring her for the last year. I'm expecting a smooth delivery."

"Good to know."

"Look." Linc drew their attention back to the horse as she lay down. "I can see the hooves."

Annie sucked a breath in. "Bets, boy or girl?"

Linc bumped her shoulder. "Filly all the way."

Allison waved her hand and said, "I'm not a part of the bet. I'm just looking for a healthy foal and mare."

"Alright, then I say it's a colt." Annie cocked her head and she saw the glint in his eye. "What are we betting?"

"If it's a girl, you cook me dinner?"

With a snort, she said, "You'd better hope it's a colt because the only thing I can make is reservations and frozen pizza."

He grinned. "Frozen pizza is my favorite."

"So... what do I get if it's a colt?"

He held up a hand. "Look. There's the nose."

Time and the bet were forgotten as she became lost in the wonder of nature in front of her. Finally with one last contraction, the foal slid out.

Allison stepped into the stall with her stethoscope in hand.

"I'm going to do a quick check of our baby and then let momma and colt bond."

"It's a colt?" Annie's heart was filled with pride. The colt's color was much like his mother's. He had his head held high as if stating to the world he had arrived.

Bowie got to her feet and began to lick and nuzzle her baby.

"Is he okay?" Annie asked.

Allison beamed. "He looks really good." She stepped out and secured the gate. "Let's go outside and give them some time together. We can check in a bit later to see him get up."

Annie slipped her hand into Linc's without thinking. Once she realized they were hand in hand, she wanted to move away but it felt good to have this connection. The sun had set in the time they had been in the barn. "That colt is a beauty and already you can see his spirit is strong."

"What are you going to name him?"

"Well, I really thought it was going to be a filly and her name would have been Bella, but now I'm thinking Beau. It's a good, strong name and I have a funny feeling he'll live up to it."

She glanced at Linc. He squeezed her hand in his and Annie thought it felt like the most natural thing in the world.

When Annie got back to the house she was exhausted. It had been quite a day, emotionally more than anything.

"Mary?" she called out as she walked in the back door, having left her boots outside. She was starving and although she knew there'd be a plate waiting for her, she would prefer company while she ate.

When she entered the kitchen, there were two places set in the breakfast nook; pots were covered on the stove, and Mary was reading in an over-stuffed chair just inside the den.

"Hey there. Did you wait on supper for me?"

"I did. I've never been a fan of eating alone and since your grandfather died, I didn't really have a meal, just picked. Now that you're home, it's time for family meals again." Mary smiled as she stood up. "Tell me about the newest addition." She looped her arm through Annie's and steered her back into the kitchen.

"He'll grow up to be a fine-looking stallion and Bowie's doing great. As soon as he was born, she was back on her feet, checking on her baby."

"I'll have to go down tomorrow and see for myself."

Annie lifted the top of a large pot and her mouth began to water when she discovered another one of her favorites, spaghetti and meatballs. "Homemade sauce?" She grabbed a slice of thick garlic bread and dunked it in the rich sauce. Before popping it in her mouth, she grinned. "What?"

Mary had a smile on her face as wide as the mountain range. "I didn't realize until this very moment how much like Pippa you are."

"Thank you. She was a great lady."

"And my best friend." Mary handed her tongs and a plate. "You don't need to stand over the stove to eat."

Annie filled a plate and handed it to Mary before taking the next one and doing the same. They got comfortable at the table and over dinner Annie filled her in on all the details of the colt. Once their plates were empty, Annie leaned back in her chair.

"Mary, can I ask you something and will you be totally honest with me?"

She arched her brow. "I will but by the look on your face, this is serious, and if you don't like my answers, please don't get angry with me."

Annie placed her hand over her heart. "I promise. But I need to know the truth about what happened the year I turned twenty-one."

Chapter Seven

"Child, what is it you want to know?" Mary wiped her mouth on the cloth napkin and set it aside.

"I talked to Linc today about when he broke it off with me. Remember it was right before I went back to school for my senior year at Boston College."

She nodded slowly. "I do remember how you cried; that boy broke your heart."

"He did and today he said he never dated much after I left, but that was the whole reason he broke it off. He wanted to date other people."

Mary gave her a long searching look. "Tell me,

how have your romantic pursuits gone while you were back East?"

"I dated, had a few romances, but nothing stuck." She toyed with her water glass. "I never met anyone who I could see standing beside me for the long haul."

"I figured as much since you never brought a man home."

Annie stacked the dirty dishes. "Is it possible I never really got over Linc and vice versa?"

With a soft laugh, Mary said, "Do ya think?"

She dropped her gaze. "That's what I thought after we got done talking earlier." But as she thought about it, her annoyance grew. "He didn't have the right to make that life-changing decision without talking to me."

"Now, think about a younger you. What would she have said if Linc broached his concerns about you staying together after graduation? You'd walk across that stage, pack your car, and head the two thousand miles back to River Junction. And what would you have done with your degree?"

"Worked with Pops. Evaluated our business and continue to make it grow."

Mary shook her head. "Now you are thinking like that young woman. Where would you have learned the skills you have today if you had come home right away? Pops knew that and he wanted you to extract all you could from life."

That made sense. Annie's knowledge of dissecting trends with any business had been honed at the firm. The bosses she'd had over the years each taught her more than she could have learned in a lifetime of running the ranch. But still…

"He also said someone wanted Pops to sell so they could develop a resort here. Do you know what that was all about?"

Mary cleared the top of the stove and started the water for tea. It was her ritual. Whenever there was an important conversation, they would have a cup of Lady Grey. Annie also knew she wouldn't start talking until she was ready.

Once the teapot was in the middle of the table, Mary drizzled honey in her cup and poured. "The developer would have shut down the real operation of the ranch and just kept parts of it for show. We would have looked like a movie set, no substance, and Pops refused to even consider the offer."

"Why didn't he say a word to me?"

"He didn't want you to worry about anything, and as far as he was concerned, it was a done deal." She took another sip while Annie absorbed the information.

"That makes no sense. He should have mentioned it in passing. I've been reviewing everything about the ranch, and we need to make some changes to be more profitable but we're not in financial trouble."

"I think now that you're back, I expect the developer, a Mr. Gasperini, to come back around. He's going to try and sway you with a wad of quick cash."

She sat back in the chair and crossed her arms over her chest. "He can try but I'm committed to keeping the Grace family legacy alive for years to come."

Mary gave her a broad smile. "Now, that's what I was hoping to hear. You might want to think about sending for the rest of your things.

You can't run this size ranch if you're not here, and no one outside the family would run it to your satisfaction, even if it was Linc."

The next morning Annie was waiting on the front porch when Polly arrived. She got out of her pickup truck and ran up the front steps.

"Good morning, Annie." She was grinning and her hazel eyes shone with excitement, her long red hair in a braid draped over one shoulder.

"Hi, Polly. Did you have any trouble finding the ranch?"

"No, and it only took about a half hour to get out here. That's always important since in July I'd want to get started early due to higher temperatures."

That was a plus; Polly understood the climate. Even though Jeremy had vouched for her, it was still a bit of an unknown if she'd be able to handle what Annie had in mind.

"Come on in the house and meet Mary. She keeps us all in line and you'll be working with her."

"Good." She rubbed her hands together. "I can't wait to see everything."

Annie held open the screen door and ushered her to the back of the house. "We're pretty informal around here, so when you're working, if you need to get a drink or use the powder room, come on in. Just leave your shoes outside." She pointed down the hall to the right. "My office is at the end of this hall and once we're outside, I'll show you the entrance from the yard too."

Polly was nodding, seeming to take it all in.

Mary stopped wiping the island when Annie and Polly came in.

"Mary Anderson, this is Polly Carson and she's here to discuss the vegetable garden."

"It's a pleasure to meet you, Mary."

She pumped her arm and Mary laughed. "Welcome to Grace Star Ranch."

"It is just beautiful out here."

Polly's eyes were twinkling and her smile genuine. It was easy to see she was sincere. Annie thought even if she wasn't great at gardening to start, she had enough enthusiasm to make up for lack of skill. This short exchange was enough for

Annie to decide she was going to give the woman a chance.

"If you're ready, I'll touch base with our cook, Quinn, and see if he can join us to talk about what his needs are. If you want to move forward, I'll have one of the ranch hands come up and we can discuss plowing up a section of land to get started."

Polly pulled out a paper from her pocket. "I jotted down some items we can plant and still get a decent harvest this year." She handed it to Annie who scanned it and passed it to Mary.

After reading the list more slowly than Annie, she said, "I'm not sure how rich the soil will be for root crops since most are heavy feeders."

Polly slipped off the small backpack she wore. Reaching in, she pulled out her hand and held up a package. "That's okay. I picked up a test kit to check the soil."

"Do you have a receipt?" Annie asked.

She shook her head. "No, it was just a few bucks."

"Polly, a few dollars can add up quick. If you pick anything up for the ranch, just submit your slips to Mary and once a week I'll cut a reimbursement check on payday. Or we have an account at the hardware store so you can charge it. I'll let Jeremy know. But all large expenses need to run through me or Rory Wilson—he's my office manager—and I'll make sure to introduce you to him before you leave today."

She nodded. "You sure have a lot of people working here."

Annie smiled. "I know I've thrown a lot of names at you, but once you meet everyone it gets easier. And besides, we need a lot of people to run the ranch. On average we have five hundred head of black angus cattle, a stable of horses, along with some chickens and pigs for our own consumption. We also grow and harvest hay to feed the animals during the winter months."

Polly gave a low whistle. "I'm gonna guess that's just scratching the surface of what goes on around here."

Mary said, "You've got that right. Ranch life is a busy one." She pushed open the back door. "Let's see about a garden."

Annie was happy to hang back and let Mary

take the lead. Before she joined the ladies, she called Quinn and let him know he should come up to the main house. Then she called Linc on the walkie to ask him who could come up and talk to Polly about getting the plot ready. He said he'd round up someone and send a man up in about a half hour.

When she walked over to Mary and Polly, they were discussing everything about composting which as far as Annie was concerned was essential for them to know but not her. She longed to go down and check on Bowie and there'd be time for that as soon as Polly was ready to start plotting the garden.

A puttering sound of the electric ATV caught her attention. Quinn was striding across the side yard to the entrance of Mary's garden.

He nodded to Mary, then said hello to Annie and Polly. He was a handsome guy and she wondered if Quinn caused the same giddy effect on women. Polly gave him a warm smile but not a hint of a flirt. Thank the stars for that.

After exchanging pleasantries, Polly handed Quinn her list of what they could grow this season, and then she withdrew another paper and handed it to him.

"This was my idea of expanding next season." She threw a look over her shoulder to Annie. "You mentioned maybe we could build a greenhouse. If we can, we could grow starter plants from seed and it would save money rather than having to buy established plants, and we'd get a jump on plant maturation."

"What are you thinking of size-wise?"

"For the garden, I'd like to start with a full acre."

His eyes widened briefly before his face returned to neutral. "That's ambitious."

She shook a hand and said, "No, I wouldn't plant it all this year, only what I'm confident we can grow—lettuce, tomatoes, cabbage. It will depend on how the soil tests, but I'd like to set up compost bins near your kitchen. Creating compost will be important and I heard a rooster so I'm guessing you have chickens too. The manure can mellow for next season too."

He laughed out loud and his bright-blue eyes danced. "Manure, we have plenty of. But sure, we can set up compost bins and a mechanism to get them dumped where you need."

"All I need to know is where can I find a tiller and to start things rolling." Polly smiled at the small group, and then her smile froze. Walking in their direction was Linc and Clint Goodman. He was Linc's right hand and a sweetheart, so why did it seem to upset Polly? That was all Annie needed—to have a personnel problem the first day Polly started work.

Clint greeted Annie with his trademark grin, showing off his deep dimples and warm dark-brown eyes. His straw cowboy hat sat squarely on his head.

"Annie, I checked on Beau before coming up. He's a handsome little colt."

He didn't show any signs of recognizing Polly so that was a positive. Maybe there wasn't going to be an issue after all.

"I'm headed down shortly."

Linc said, "Mind if I join you?"

His deep voice caused a flutter in her belly. Some things never changed. "Sure."

Clint hugged Mary, but his eyes were on Polly. "Hello."

She gave him a small wave. "Hi, I'm Polly Carson."

He kept one arm around Mary's shoulders and dipped his head. "Nice to meet you."

Annie said, "Clint, I'd like for you to work with Polly today"—she glanced at Linc—"and tomorrow if she needs help getting the ground ready to plant. I'm sure Linc told you my plans."

"He did." He focused his attention solely on Polly. "I'll follow your lead."

"Great." The word came out as a squeak.

Mary said, "Well, I'll be in the house if anyone needs me."

Taking the cue, Quinn headed back to his ATV and said if Polly needed lunch to head to the dining hall.

Annie was pleased to see he welcomed her with the simple invitation. Quinn was a funny kind of a guy. You never knew which way the wind would blow with him. But he was good at his job and his food was excellent.

Linc said, "Do you need to do any office work

or are you free to take a run down to check on the horses?"

Annie saw Clint and Polly were already talking about her plans and she was pleased to see Polly had her easy smile again.

She said to Linc, "I'm all yours." Sometimes she wished she would think about what she was going to say before she actually said it.

He beamed. "Can I hold you to that?"

She shook her head. "Linc... you know what I meant."

He winked. "But are you sure how you meant it?"

Chapter Eight

Annie gave Linc a nudge. "I'll walk down to the barn so go ahead with the ATV."

He flashed her a knowing look. "Is that your way of telling me you need some space, but you'll meet me there?"

He caught her. When Linc was around, it clouded her thoughts and pulled her back to the way she felt about him; it was confusing. She believed that their romance was long since over, but she could tell he felt the pull too.

"Why waste time to walk with me up and back when after we're done in the barn you can take off and go back to work?" She patted her backside. "I've been doing too much sitting and eating way too much of Mary's delicious food. I need the exercise."

"Anytime you want to work up a good sweat, just let me know."

She stopped midstep. Had he just propositioned her?

His face flushed a deep shade of red. "I mean, there are always stalls to muck and ranch work to be done. It burns tons of calories."

"Um. Thanks for the offer." She wouldn't admit it to Linc, but the original thought was very tempting and the way he blushed was downright sexy.

They walked in silence, occasionally bumping arms.

"Have you seen any wolves around the ranch yet?"

"No, are we having a problem?" Part of a rancher's reality was wolves picking off livestock.

"We lost a few calves this spring, but it's been kind of quiet lately. Hopefully they're hunting farther up the mountains." He gave her a sharp look. "I know you haven't been out riding yet, but do me a favor when you do. Make sure you tell someone and take at least a pistol with you. I'd hate for you to be caught off guard."

"I'll remember that. The worst I've seen so far is a couple of spiders in the yard. But thanks for your concern."

He touched her hand. "Some things will never change, Annie."

The way he said her name was like a soft breeze off the plains and there was nothing more she wanted to do than throw her arms around his neck and kiss him. But she had emotions to sort through; was this simply a reaction to being home? Nostalgia?

"Tell me about my girl. Did you swing by Bowie's stall before you came up to the house?"

"Can't pull anything over on you. But momma and colt are amazing. He's nursing well and he's got his legs under him. He really is handsome."

"I'm looking forward to taking her out for a ride when she's ready. Maybe you'd like to join me?"

He didn't hesitate before saying, "I'll make the time."

Dang it. She was offering him an olive branch and he just made it seem like it was part of his job.

She got to the barn door first and slid it open and quickly walked away from Linc. He had a way of making her blood boil and this time it wasn't for a pleasant reason.

"Annie, wait." He jogged to catch up to her, his boots clicking on the cement floor. "What did I say?"

"Nothing." She slowed her steps as she grew closer to Bowie's stall. She patted her pockets and realized she didn't grab any apples or carrots. She'd come back down later and bring two.

He handed her an apple from a bucket next to the stall door. "Here."

She nodded her thanks and focused her attention on momma and baby. "Hey, girl." Bowie's ears twitched at the sound of her voice and she nickered softly. "I've got a treat for you."

She ambled a few steps in her direction and Beau was glued to her flank. Annie reached out and scratched her velvety soft nose. She then held out her other hand with the apple. Bowie's lips brushed the apple, and then her teeth crunched down. Juice dribbled to the ground. Annie couldn't help but laugh at her delicate motion.

"I'm sorry it took a while to get down here today." She ran her hand down her neck and gave it a few pats. Without looking at Linc, she said, "Bowie looks good."

Linc was standing beside her. "She does. Doc Howard will be by later to check on both of them."

"Good." She wanted to clear the air but wasn't sure how best to do that. She could hear Pippa's voice in her head. *Just apologize.* She glanced his way, but he was focused on the horses.

"Polly seems very enthusiastic." This was a safe topic. "I'm hopeful she's going to fit in around here, but did you see the look she gave Clint? Do you know of any bad blood between them?"

"Clint? He doesn't have an enemy anywhere on earth. He's a good guy, shoots straight, and likes everyone."

"That's what I always thought, but when she laid eyes on him, she seemed to be tongue-tied."

"He's not a bad-looking guy from what I can see unless you say different. Maybe they'd bumped into each other in the past."

"That's not it. They greeted each other as strangers, and I don't think you can fake that kind of reaction."

She continued to rub Bowie's nose as Beau hugged closer to her side. Annie wanted to reach out, but the colt was skittish. She just left her arm hanging until his curiosity got the best of him. Bonding with Beau was going to be a slow process but once he accepted her as the head of his herd, he'd be devoted.

"You have good instincts with him, never pushing, waiting for him to come to you."

"Pops always said it was important to take the time with animals and people to let them get accustomed to you before charging forward. Beau and I will be best buds in no time at all. I just need to make sure I'm down here daily. Besides it'll give me an excuse to get out of the office." She gave him a smile. "It's possible we might even bump into each other on a more regular basis."

His smile widened. "I like the sound of that." He stretched his hand out to her, and then he seemed to change his mind and patted Bowie's side.

They stayed a bit longer before Annie said she needed to get back up to the house. Walking in a companionable silence, they stayed in step with each other. Once they got to where Linc had parked the ATV, she wanted to say something.

"Thanks for sending Clint over to help out."

"No need to thank me; he works for you."

"Well, yes and no. He has responsibilities for you and I'm guessing I put you in a bind with chores." She scuffed the toe of her boot in the dirt, causing little clouds of dust to kick up.

"Don't give it another thought. We've got enough people to pitch in and besides, everyone's excited about the idea of the garden and becoming more independent in the winter months. This homegrown stuff has come full circle with people."

Now she couldn't help but laugh. "You sound

like some old fuddy-duddy with the new city slicker ideas of organic gardening and sustainability."

"Buzz words. The truth is we like simple but good food and Quinn provides that for us. If we eat healthier and enjoy it more, all the better."

He got on the ATV. "I'm gonna take off so if you need something or find you want some company when you go back down to the barn, just holler. I'll be in the office for the rest of the day. I've got a few things to go over with Rory."

She nodded and pointed to the house. "You know where I'll be too."

She waited until he drove away and turned onto the access road. With a heavy heart, she wandered around the side of the house to enter her office from the back. The air hung heavy with the promise of much-needed rain. She thought of Polly and Clint getting ready to turn over a plot of land. She detoured to where she thought they'd be to see how things were going. In reality, she was stalling. It felt good to be out walking the land.

She'd have to make a point to do this a few times a day. She might even see if her old bicycle was still around so she could bike around the property until Bowie was up for a ride.

The garden was to be situated halfway between the main house and the dining hall. Annie could see Polly with a large brimmed hat in her hand and Clint driving the tractor with the plow attachment. He would make short work of tilling the space. As she approached, she could see the smile on Polly's face was a mile wide. This was definitely her element.

"Hey, how's it going here?" Annie stood next to her, watching Clint turn when he got to the end of the garden.

"I hope this is an okay place for the garden. I just realized I should have checked with you first."

Annie paused and looked around. Wide-open space, plenty of sun, near water.

"I can guarantee it won't be an unsightly mess when you sit on the back patio."

Annie looked over her shoulder in the direction of the house. "I hadn't even given that a thought but now that you mention it, I will be able to see the garden from my office. I'm thinking we should have an attractive fence around it. Split rail maybe?"

"That won't keep the critters out that might want to nibble on what we're growing."

Annie could sense Polly relax as she talked. "Well, it could work if we added some green plastic fencing on the inside to the posts and a gate. But that'll be more work. I mean I could do it; I've installed fence posts before but..." Her voice trailed off.

"Figure up what we'll need and talk to Linc. He can get a few guys in to make short work of it. He can even handle getting materials ordered. While you're at it, ask him to give Rory your list for tools and any other supplies. Once this is dug up and the fencing is finished, the bigger equipment won't be able to get in."

She beamed. "I'll put it together tonight and give it to Linc tomorrow. And don't worry, I'll keep everything reasonable."

She liked this girl even more. She wasn't

looking to spend frivolously. "I appreciate you being cost-conscious, but I'm a firm believer in having the proper equipment to get the job done."

"Thanks, Annie. I won't disappoint you."

She laughed. "I'm expecting you to feed us all. That's a huge responsibility."

Polly's smile dimmed a bit, like a cloud flitted over her sunshine. "I'm up to the challenge."

After a few more minutes of talking about her plans, Annie walked back to the house after reminding Clint to take Polly in for lunch soon before all the guys made it in. Well, at least those near enough to eat.

Mary was puttering in her small kitchen garden when Annie saw her.

"What do you think of our new hire?" She perched on a butt-high raised bed which helped Mary from having to work bent over. At her age, north of seventy, she could use a little extra ease in life. She'd been working and living here for the last fifty years, after her husband died in a freak accident on the ranch. Her grandmother and Mary had been best friends in school so Pippa made sure she had a soft place to land.

"I like her. It's easy to see she's got a strong work ethic; her arms are toned which you only get from honest work or in a gym and based on her golden tan she spends a lot of time outdoors."

She continued to turn over the soil around the lettuce plants and then plucked a slug off and tossed it into the coffee can at her feet. "Darn bugs."

"Polly's gonna put up a fence around the new garden. Linc will have to bring in some extra hands to get it done in a day. Clint wouldn't be able to get that done by himself and I need him back doing his regular job."

"That won't need to get done this week even if you can get all the supplies here. There's plenty of time. Polly's got her hands full just prepping the soil to grow anything."

"And before the fence goes up, they'll need to drop in manure."

Mary brushed her hands off on her jeans and set her tools aside. "Composted manure if there's any still out near the barn. Rory's been selling the excess to the garden center out off Highway One."

All these details she had no idea about. It was a good thing Mary seemed to know what was going on at the ranch. "Is there anything you don't know about what's going on around here?"

The older woman grinned broadly. "If it's worth knowing, then I got my finger on the pulse."

Annie laughed loudly. "Good to know."

"With that confession, how about I rustle us up a little lunch. You've got office work to do this afternoon."

"Did you keep Pops on the straight and narrow too?"

"Child, you have no idea when it came to your grandfather how easily he could get diverted. He'd rather get his hands dirty than deal with the paperwork, but it's the price of being the owner."

"And now that's me." She slipped her hand through the crook of Mary's arm. "My only hope is I'm as good a leader as he was."

"Stay humble, put the people who work for you first, always before profits." Mary hugged her arm tight. "You're so much like him and I know for a fact he never doubted your ability to fill his boots."

She blinked away the tears that threatened to spill down her cheeks. Mary telling her she was like Pops was the greatest compliment she had ever heard.

"Thank you, Mary. I'll do my best."

She paused and looked out over the endless acreage of Grace land. "Trust your intuition. It will never steer you wrong."

Did Mary know something she wasn't telling her?

Chapter Nine

Annie could feel the heavy weight of responsibility for the ranch sitting squarely on her shoulders every time she sat in Pops' desk chair. The ranch started at the glass door and ended somewhere far beyond what she could see, and it had been passed for her to keep a steady hand and continue to grow it for the next generation. But who would care for the ranch when she was gone? That was a problem for another day. Right now she had work to do.

She opened her email and scanned the new messages. Some were standard bills, upcoming auctions, but one caused her to stop scanning and actually open it. It was from J and B Trust. Could this be the same company that had approached Pops? She should have asked Linc the company's name.

Dear Ms. Price,

I would like to meet with you to discuss the future of Grace Star Ranch. You may have been made aware that I spoke with your grandfather several months ago, but my company is still very interested in your property. I believe a conversation would be mutually beneficial to both parties.

Please let me know when it would be convenient for us to meet. My main office is in San Francisco, but I would be happy to meet you at Grace Star Ranch.

Sincerely,
Lucas Gasperini, Project Lead
Crystal Resorts Development

Annie read the email a second time. There wasn't much to glean from a few sentences. She pushed back from the desk and opened the sliding door before sitting in her grandmother's rocking chair.

It had brought her comfort since she'd been back, a good place for deep thinking.

She rested her head on the back of the chair and closed her eyes, channeling Pops to tell her what to expect from Mr. Gasperini. She had no intention of selling the ranch. This was her home and if anyone was going to expand into a resort type of ranch, she would do it. She didn't need a fat check. The longer she was home, the more her soul relaxed and reconnected with the rhythm of life here.

Her cell rang and it was a special tone she had set for Daphne. She answered it before it would go to voicemail. Before Annie could say hello, she was already talking.

"What's a BFF got to do to get a phone call from the newest hotshot rancher in Montana?"

With a laugh, Annie said, "And what does a rancher have to do to get a call from the premier event planner in the city of Boston?"

Daphne Brenner had become like a sister to Annie when they met at boarding school in Massachusetts and they both attended college in Boston so it was easy to stay close. Daphne's family lived in New York City so on short school breaks Annie had gone home with her instead of staying at school. Then after they graduated college, they shared an apartment in Boston before snipping the cord and getting separate places but in the same neighborhood.

"Touché. Gosh, Annie, it's been almost a month since we've talked. What's going on out there? Are you ready to head back to the coast and get a proper seafood dinner instead of all that beef?"

"No, I don't think I am." She savored the view. "I'm home and I don't want to leave."

"Wow, that wasn't what I expected you to say. What have you been doing since you've been back? And the most important question, did you actually unpack?"

She had to laugh. The question wasn't about tidiness, but if she had settled in. "Not only did I unpack, but I put my suitcases in the back of the closet."

"This is serious. Tell me everything that's going on."

Annie heard a thump. "Did you just put your feet on the desk and settle in to chat?"

"Absolutely. We have a lot to catch up on. Starting with, have you seen your hunk?"

There was no reason to question who she was referring to. Linc had been the topic of many conversations over the last fifteen plus years. "We bump into each other almost daily." She thought of his intense hazel eyes and the way he watched her when they were together. "It's been nice to catch up."

"I'm sensing there's more to that story." She paused, but Annie didn't elaborate. "What projects have you launched? I know before you left you were working on some ideas."

"I've hired a girl from town to put in a huge vegetable garden. My plan is to feed the ranch hands seasonal food and even have enough to preserve for winters."

"That's ambitious. Someone you knew from before?"

"No, but you'd like her. Polly's full of energy and ideas, and I think she'll be a good fit long term. I'm even thinking of putting up a greenhouse next year if this goes well."

"And how's Mary? Same as ever?"

"Keeping us all in line. She's getting older and a little slower but still has an opinion about everything, and she voices it when she sees an opening. I can't believe it, but she's got to be pushing eighty."

"Sounds like someone I'd like to emulate when I get up there in age." Daphne laughed softly.

Annie wished they were sitting on the porch together. She had always been a good sounding board. "Remember my horse, Bowie?"

"Yeah, how's the old girl?"

"She had a foal, and I've named him Beau. He's beautiful."

"You didn't mention anything about increasing the stable."

She smiled. "I didn't know. My grandfather bred her last year and never told me. And when I was here for the end, I never went out to the barn. Pops had been my sole focus those last days."

"Understandable but what a nice surprise for

you. It's like a bit of him lives on in a way through the colt."

They spent the next few minutes talking about mutual friends and when Annie might be back in Boston. She decided to talk to Daphne about Lucas Gasperini.

"So something odd happened. I got an email today from a real estate developer out of San Francisco. He wants to meet with me about the ranch."

"Do you think he heard about your grandfather passing away and is going to swoop in for a fast and cheap deal?"

"Linc told me Pops already handled this guy so I'm not sure why he's coming back around. I guess he wants to open up a resort with the ranch still sort of working."

"How do you feel about that?"

"Like it's a nonstarter. I don't want to sell. This place is all I have left of my family. Besides, I have a responsibility to the people who've worked for Pops for years. Working a ranch is like a big family and I was raised you never walk away from them."

"Does that mean you're going to take a meeting with this guy?"

She sighed. Annie knew what she had to do. "At least a courtesy phone call. Hopefully that will end his pursuit of my land."

"Is there anything I can do to help?"

Annie could picture Daphne standing in four-inch heels and her tailored suit, giving Mr. Gasperini a what for, right before she told him to beat feet. "No. I've got this but if I need to call in reinforcements, you're at the top of the list."

"Right behind a handsome ranch hand?"

"He's the manager of the place. Everyone reports to him—well, except me and Mary." She laughed. "But I'm pretty sure Mary runs this place. I don't think there is one ranch hand on this spread that wouldn't defer to her if they had to."

"Is that because you're close?"

"Heck no. I think it's because she's lived and worked here for longer than most of my people have been alive, me included."

"Annie, you know what I like about you?"

"That I can fix a mean martini?" She smiled.

She hadn't fixed any kind of a drink since she'd been here.

"Well, that but you don't call the people who work for you employees. You refer to them as your family, your people. It shows how much you care and if Mr. Gasperini would hear how you talk about your home and everyone who surrounds you, he'd know he should look elsewhere."

"Thanks, Daph. That was just what I needed to hear."

"Anytime. Now the most important question, is my room ready for my arrival?"

Annie squealed. "When are you coming? I'll pick you up from the airport. Make sure you fly into Bozeman. It's the closest major airport unless you want to take a small plane from there and I can pick you up outside of town. One of the neighboring ranches has a small airstrip."

"Hold on there. I just asked if you were ready for visitors, not that I had booked my ticket yet. But I would like to take a couple of weeks and come out if that'd be okay with you."

"You can stay as long as you like. But don't

you have events to plan? Wedding season is right around the corner."

Daphne grew silent. Annie could wait until she was ready to talk.

A long minute ticked by, and then she said, "I'm burned out. I'm leaving Oceanside Events."

This didn't sound right; Daphne loved events. But she had a suspicion there was something more involved.

"What aren't you telling me?"

"It's no big deal."

This time Annie could hear her voice waver. "Tell me. Maybe I can help."

"You know Chad's parents own the business and we broke up two weeks ago. So, I don't want to stay there and bump into him all the time."

"Did they fire you?" Her temper spiked at the thought of the Dunhams being so petty.

"This is my decision. I've turned over all remaining events to another planner. It's okay. I've been there for ten years. Maybe I'll start my own company after I get back to Boston."

"Well, just so you know, I have plenty of room and you can stay as long as you like. You'll have a roof over your head, and Mary will take care of all the cooking. It'll be like your very own dude ranch experience, minus the spa."

"Sounds like a slice of heaven." She laughed softly. "Maybe we can get in a trail ride or two and I can finally meet your handsome cowboy."

"Maybe."

She could hear Daph's hands clap together. "I knew it. The old flame has been rekindled. Now I really can't wait to meet him."

"Daphne, you're incorrigible. Let's talk next week and make some firm plans. You'll also need to pack for cooler weather. It gets chilly here at night."

"Sounds good. Annie, I'm glad you sound so happy, but I miss you."

She swallowed the lump that rose in her throat. She hadn't realized how much she missed Daphne until this call. "I miss you too. Call me back once you've booked your ticket."

"Deal."

After they said goodbye, Annie wandered into the house in search of Mary. She wanted to talk about which room would be best for Daphne when she came. She was planning for her to stay indefinitely. And before she arrived, Annie had some decisions to make. Maybe Daphne could relocate to Montana and find a position here at Grace Star. It'd be nice to have her best friend around.

After a walk through the house, Annie looked out the front window to see if Mary's car was around. But since it wasn't, she figured the older woman had gone to town or maybe even to her book club.

Back in her office, Annie pulled up the email from the developer. Instead of returning the email, she decided to give him a call. No sense putting off what she could handle right now and put it behind her.

"Crystal Resorts Development, this is Joanne. How may I help you?"

Well, it sounded like a professional organization by the way the phone was answered. "Hello, this is Annie Grace and I'm trying to reach Lucas Gasperini. Is he available?"

"One moment, please."

She was placed on hold with typical instrumental music with songs from the fifties and sixties. While she waited she doodled on the pad in front of her. The next several minutes crawled by and the receptionist nor Gasperini picked up the phone. She'd give them one more minute of her time before she hung up.

"Ms. Grace, this is Lucas Gasperini. I must say, this is an unexpected surprise."

His voice was smooth and practiced. He must have to answer the phone this way on a regular basis.

"Hello, Mr. Gasperini. I received an email from you regarding my ranch, Grace Star."

"Thank you for calling me back. I'm sure you must be dealing with a great deal considering your grandfather's passing. He was a fine man."

Now she just wanted to gag. He acted as if he and Pops had been buds.

When she didn't bother to respond to his last comment, he said, "I would like to come out to Montana, or I could fly you to San Francisco and we could discuss the sale of your ranch to my company. We'd love to build a very special vacation destination in Montana and after careful consideration, all parties have decided that your land is the prime choice. The river running through it has some of the best trout fishing in the state."

She rolled her eyes as if she didn't know about the spectacular points about her ranch. Before he could go any further, Annie said, "What makes you think I'd be interested in selling?"

"Ms. Grace, or may I call you Annie?"

Now she was getting annoyed. She hated slick salesmen, and this was definitely a sales pitch. "Ms. Grace is fine."

"I've taken the liberty to learn a bit more about you and I've discovered you're a business analyst. A keen mind will comprehend the significance of an offer such as this. I'd be happy to share our research with you and perhaps even sweeten the offer with a slice of the profits."

The pencil she had been doodling with snapped in half between her fingers. Tossing it aside, she wondered if he was implying Pops didn't understand what Gasperini was peddling.

"I don't think a meeting will tell me anything

I don't already know. Grace Star Ranch isn't for sale now, just as it wasn't when my grandfather was alive."

"But Ms. Grace. As a young woman, do you want to be tied to a tract of land? Wouldn't you be more comfortable back in your townhouse in Boston?"

"I see you've been very thorough in your research, but I can assure you, my answer is no."

"Why don't you take a week or so and think about it and I'd be happy to come to you."

She took a slow, deep breath. This man was like a dog with a meaty bone. "Thank you for your interest, but I won't change my mind, Mr. Gasperini."

She disconnected the phone after he tried one more time to convince her to think it over. Tossing the phone on the desk, she flung open the glass door. The only thing that would cure her sour mood was a trip to see Bowie and her baby. Who said she wasn't a rancher from the top of her head to her toes?

Chapter Ten

In the last two weeks Linc hadn't spent much time with Annie but not for lack of wanting to. She seemed to stay pretty busy, and he saw her working with Polly in the garden a few times. In some ways it was great to see her outside, but he did worry if she was neglecting ranch business. Pops had a schedule. Either the morning or afternoon was spent in his office, and from what he could tell, Annie didn't have any sort of a schedule. It made him wonder how she had been successful at her job in Boston.

Or maybe that was the rub; she was planning to go back and this was more like a vacation to her. His heart dropped deep to his gut. He couldn't stand to think he wasn't going to see her every day. It had been too many years of wishing he had done things differently. If he could go back in time, he'd never have broken it off with her. He'd been young and dumb, a guy trying to be noble. After all, it was part of who he was, a man who put others ahead of himself. But for Annie, he'd do anything to ensure she was happy.

She was skipping down the front steps when he drove by the lower driveway. He stopped the truck and waited for her to catch up. Beautiful as always, dressed in a sleeveless cotton blouse, with just tight enough jeans and work boots. In her hand she carried a large woven hat.

She leaned in the open window and pulled her large sunglasses low. "Hey, you. Where are you going in such a hurry? I could see the clouds of dust from the house."

He'd like to say he was in a hurry to see her. But that wasn't just today; it was every day. He pushed that thought aside.

"Off to get lunch. Wanna come along?"

"I could eat." She opened the door and

hopped in the passenger door. "I haven't seen you much. I guess you've been busy."

"I could say the same about you. Anything special you've been working on?"

She gave him a wide smile. "I've cleaned out my closet and got rid of some clothes that should have gone to the thrift store ages ago. Oh, and Mary and I got the guest room ready for my friend Daphne. Do you remember her? She came out to the funeral and has been here a few other times over the years. Short redhead with a smattering of freckles on her face."

He remembered her. She had a strong New England accent right down to the way she said quarter. For some reason she continued to drop the first *R* and it bugged him. Thank heavens Annie hadn't picked up that bad habit.

He grinned. "I do. Is she coming out?"

"I hope so. She needs a change of scene and I said she should fly in and stay a while. The ranch has restorative powers, almost magical."

He adjusted the cowboy hat on his head and smiled. "That it does." He dropped the truck in gear and drove more slowly to the long low building that housed the kitchen, dining hall, general bunkhouse, and a few offices, including his and Rory's. There was room for a couple more people if Annie wanted to move down. Not that he'd suggest it; that was overstepping. She could work wherever she wanted.

After he parked, they climbed the stone stairs, their footsteps in sync. Like every building on the ranch, this had been built to last for generations. Pops added on to it when he had suggested they hire more ranch hands, not because they needed the space but to design them more like apartments, where there were common areas and then the bunk rooms. It gave them an edge when compared to other ranches. He wanted to talk to Annie about building a few more cabins too. Some of the guys were in serious relationships and it'd be better to have cabins here in case they decided to get married. They could offer housing for a couple, and if they decided to have families, that would be a different story.

Annie jabbed him in the side. "Hey, you invited me to lunch and it implies conversation."

"Sorry. Got lost in thought." He pulled open

a heavy wooden door and stepped to one side so she could enter.

The minute she was inside, she inhaled. "OMG. What is Quinn making? My mouth is already watering."

"Well, it's Wednesday which means clean out the walk-in day. You're in for a real treat. The things he can do with a little bit of this and a lot of that will show you just how talented he is."

"I looked in his file when I was reviewing things, and there's not much about his background. What do you know about him?"

Linc stopped walking and Annie did the same. "He's kind of a private guy, like most around here. Even the ones who think they're comedians, and we respect that."

She blinked hard. "I wasn't looking for idle gossip. I own the ranch and these men work for me. If there is something in their background that is important for me to know, it should be in their file."

He exhaled before speaking. It was best to let go of his temper before he spoke. A lesson he had learned long ago. "Then maybe you should have a conversation with him and get to know the rest of the men. It would go a long way for them to see the person behind the signature on their paychecks."

Her cheeks flushed pink. "I think I'll skip lunch."

The kitchen door opened, and Quinn came out carrying a large covered pot. He eyed them both and Linc wondered if he could feel the tension in the air.

"Annie, Linc. You're just in time." He flashed Annie a grin. "If I'd known you were coming, I would have made something a little fancier than soup."

Gracious as always, she gave him a warm smile. "I was going to head up to the house."

The smile dimmed. He said, "Sure, no problem."

"But now that I'm here and it does smell delicious, I'd love to have a bowl."

Quinn said, "I just need to get the biscuits and a few other things, and I'll be right back."

He left the room, leaving Linc and Annie in an awkward silence.

She wiped her hands on the back of her jeans. "I'm going to see if I can help."

He gave a curt nod. "I'll go check email. I'll be back."

They parted ways and he strode into his office. He took off his hat and ran his hand through his hair. That woman was enough to send him on a long trail ride with nothing but his horse and a bed roll. He wanted to kiss her senseless and then yell at her for being a city snob. Did she really think she could learn about the people who worked for her by reading a file? Some of the men who worked here had a scrape or two before driving through the gate.

He plunked down in his chair and leaned on his knees. He did think she'd be better off getting to know everyone. A few of the guys were happy to see the new garden going in. It gave them hope they had a future here. He'd have to point out to her again why it was important to get to know everyone. He was certain of one thing; she had spent way too much time living in a city and she forgot what it was like to be a member of a small-town ranch community.

Heck, she hadn't even gone into town except the time they went and that was a couple of weeks ago.

He fired up his computer to do as he said, check email. Not that she'd ever know if he had lied, but he would know and that was all that mattered.

Laughter drifted into his office and Linc glanced at the clock on the screen. He had gotten sucked in and a half hour had passed. He had to wonder if Annie had stayed or if she went back to the main house. He shut the computer down and made it back to the main hall in record time. He was pleasantly surprised to see Annie sitting at one of the long banquet tables with about ten of the guys sitting around her. He paused to listen to the laughter, and he was happy to see she was beaming.

She looked up and said, "Linc, you'd better get over here and get a bowl of Quinn's Wednesday Soup. It was amazing."

He strolled to where the food was laid out and he could see the pot was only about a third full. It must have been good. He filled a bowl, grabbed three thick biscuits, and walked back to the tables where he was going to sit down at one by himself.

Annie said, "Come over here."

She slid down, leaving just barely enough room for him to squeeze in between her and Zak. It figured the horse wrangler would capture her attention. He was probably sharing stories about her beloved Bowie and baby. He didn't take time to examine his gut reaction to the situation.

"Thanks." He gave Zak a pointed look.

"Not a problem, boss." He gave Linc plenty of elbow room to spread out. "I was just tellin' Annie that Beau is going to be quite the handful when it comes time to start trainin' him."

"I'll be training him." Linc buttered a biscuit and took a bite, not tasting it.

"Oh. I didn't know that was the plan," Zak stuttered. "I, well, I was just talking about his spunk."

If Annie caught the undertone to his voice, she didn't react but it was just as well. She was talking to Rory about how long he'd been at the ranch.

One by one the cowboys picked up their

empty bowls and plates and indicated they were getting back to work. Quinn came out of the kitchen with a platter of cookies, which was something he did every Wednesday. Linc thought it was to offset serving them what he considered leftovers, but they definitely weren't his momma's. He smiled to himself. Heck, you couldn't even eat his momma's meals the first time.

"What caused that look on your face?" Annie leaned in and took half of his buttered biscuit.

"Just thinking about my mother."

She frowned. "Memories of my mom have faded over the years. It's been so long since the plane crash. I only really remember the big moments."

He placed his large hand over her small one; her skin was soft like rose petals. "I wish I had the chance to get to know them."

"My dad was like Pops, but in a younger form. Adventurous, kind, and hard-working to a fault. And Mom was right by his side, working as hard as he did."

"That's why they were together."

She nodded and finished for him. "When the

plane went down." She looked around. "We're the only two left."

"Everyone has work to do." He spooned up more of the thick, rib-sticking soup. "So what did you think of your first Quinn meal?"

"He could give any chef a serious run for their money if he can do this with leftovers. I can't wait to see what he makes for a real meal."

Linc scraped the bottom of the bowl. "Maybe you should tell him that. It'd go a long way."

She gave him a quizzical look. "Why are you encouraging me to talk to my guys? It's not like I'm gonna disappear or anything."

He cocked a brow. "How do they know that? You haven't lived on the ranch in a very long time. Maybe they're all wondering if being home will make you fall in love with the place so you'll want to stay."

"I do love this place. These are my roots."

"Then why have you stayed away? Even when Pops got sick, you didn't come back until the end."

"I came home for the holidays when I could, and he never said he was sick. He explained his weight loss by trying to get into better shape. He sold me a bill of goods and I bought it. So, get off your high horse, Linc, and stop thinking that I am some horrible granddaughter who didn't give flying cow chips about him. I loved Pops; he was the only family I had in the world. Do you really think if I had known he was dying I would have stayed away? Only when Mary told me what was happening did I understand he had been keeping the truth from me. Pops thought he was doing the right thing, but when I got here, I spent as much time as I could, storing every memory of our time together to last me a lifetime." She pushed her chair back so hard it fell over with a bang. "For the record, I recorded his jokes, stories, and songs on my phone so he'll always be with me."

Tears filled her eyes and instantly he regretted what he had said and implied. She picked up her dishes and set them back down before she ran out the door. He hesitated half a minute before following her.

"Annie, wait. I'm sorry." The next words died on his lips when he saw a fancy sedan pulling up next to his truck. His gut tightened. Who was behind the wheel? Someone from Annie's adopted hometown?

She wiped her cheeks dry with the back of her hand and plastered on a cautious smile as she waited on the top step.

A short man in a dark pinstriped suit and lapis-blue tie got out from behind the wheel. He looked between Annie and Linc.

"Hello. I'm wondering if you could tell me where I would find Annie Grace? I knocked on the door at the house, but no one answered."

Linc took a step forward to be by Annie's side.

She didn't react to him standing next to her. "You found her. And who are you?"

He gave her a wide smile. It reminded Linc of a predator stalking its dinner.

"I'm Lucas Gasperini and I was hoping you might spare some time for me."

Linc dropped his voice. "Did you know he was coming?"

She stepped forward and said, "This is unexpected. I have a few minutes to spare." She gestured to the wide porch. "Let's talk here, shall we?"

He walked up the steps and gave Linc a curt nod.

Annie looked at Linc. "Would you have time to join us?"

"I'd be happy to." Now what did this snake want? With Annie's cool façade, he had no idea which way the winds were going to blow.

Chapter Eleven

Annie sat on a handcrafted wooden rocking chair. It was one of the things she liked best about this ranch. Everything had a sturdy feel to it and she needed something solid under her since she was still reeling from her disagreement with Linc just moments before.

Mr. Gasperini had pulled his pocket square from his breast pocket and patted his face and neck. "It's warm today."

Since she didn't ask for the meeting, there was no sense in making it easy on him. She hated it when people just showed up. She felt as if it was invading her personal space. Linc had taken a chair so he could see both her and Lucas's faces. He was shrewd and sure to not miss a single thing.

"How may I help you, Mr. Gasperini?" She was doing her best to assert her authority, not that she needed to. After all, she held all the cards he was interested in.

"Please, call me Lucas." He handed her his business card and as if in afterthought, he gave one to Linc. He didn't look at it but stuck it in his shirt pocket.

She gave him a half nod but didn't say anything else. This was his show, let him work for it.

He opened his briefcase, pulled out a manila folder, and handed Annie an envelope. She took it.

"Annie."

She didn't like that he took the liberty of calling her by her first name. It made things seem too familiar somehow. But rather than correct him and make things really awkward, she let it go.

"In that envelope contains a very generous offer, more than what I had originally offered your grandfather for Grace Star Ranch."

She cocked one brow and said, "Really? And why would you sweeten the pot?"

He leaned forward as if they were about to be overheard. "I am so sorry for your loss, and I know he was your last surviving family member. I wanted to make sure you were taken care of."

She looked at the envelope, not in the least bit interested in what the contents were. She measured her words carefully. "I appreciate the gesture but as I said on the phone, I'm not interested in selling Grace Star."

She didn't make a move to get up but waited to see what he would say next. Out of the corner of her eye, she could see Linc clasp his hands, his knuckles white. She wanted to fill him in on what she was thinking, but now wasn't the time. No sense in tipping her hand when there was more to learn from the overbearing developer.

He reached back into his briefcase and for half a second she was reminded of Santa pulling presents from his sack, but this was not Christmas and he was definitely not Kris Kringle. This time he handed her a thin binder.

"I think you'll find my research to be enlightening." He gave her a smarmy smile. "I know you deal with facts and figures, and I thought if I showed you what we had in mind, it would put you at ease and understand the essence of the ranch would remain. We would just be building on what was already here to give a wide group of people the opportunity to enjoy what you have."

Lucas Gasperini reminded Annie of a slime-ball from an old movie, but the report intrigued her. He had just given her another stepping stone in her own plan. She quickly skimmed the pages and withheld the smile that threatened to fill her face. This was excellent work. Whoever had done the research broke everything down. But why wasn't Lucas worried she'd take the information and run with it on her own? Based on her experience, he should be.

Keeping her poker face in place, she said, "I'll look this over." Remaining cool was hard when all she wanted to do was start at page one and take lots of notes to build upon what he handed her.

"Would it be possible to walk around a bit? I'd love to see more of your ranch."

Without hesitation, she said, "We can take a

golf cart since there would be too much to cover on foot." She glanced at his highly polished Allen Edmonds shoes. Annie knew from her boss they were the best mass-produced shoes without buying custom in the United States and at a somewhat reasonable price.

He placed his hand over his chest. "Oh good. I'm a little overdressed for an outdoor meeting."

"It is a warm today." She looked at Linc. "What, eighty-eight?"

He gave her a curt nod. "Something like that."

The frosty edge in his voice caught her by surprise. He didn't have to like Gasperini any more than she did, but where was his tone coming from?

"Would you like a glass of water before we head out?"

Linc flashed her a quizzical look.

"That would be nice, thank you."

Annie got up and said, "I'll be right back."

Linc was right behind her without even acknowledging the visitor as he walked in front of him. He grabbed her arm once they were inside, out of sight.

"What do you think you're doing?"

The gold in his eyes didn't sparkle and the hazel was a dull brown. What was his problem? She looked down where he held her arm and then back at him. He released it.

"Being polite."

"But showing him around, letting him get a closer look at our operation?"

"What's the harm in listening to his ideas?" Now she was getting annoyed. Linc was speaking to her as if she were a child or worse someone who had no idea what they were doing.

"The harm? He just gave you some kind of an offer that he thinks will make you pull out a pen and sign on the dotted line so you can jet off to Boston and live the rest of your life in luxury."

"Just because I have some papers, that means that I...?" Before she could finish her question, Linc turned and stormed out of the hall in the direction of his office.

He called over his shoulder, "I can't talk to you right now."

She stood open-mouthed, wondering what his issue was. She was on a fact-finding mission and knew exactly how to handle Lucas Gasperini or anyone else like him that came along. With a shake of her head, she poured a glass of water from the pitcher and went back to the front porch. She was going to enjoy showing off her ranch to this over-confident schmooze.

Annie drove Gasperini past the cabins, near the barns, into a small pasture where the horses were grazing, and even to where the river ran closer to the house. On their way back to his car, she noticed he was still grinning from ear to ear, like a cat who got the extra plump bird.

"What did you think of my little spread?" She wanted to make it clear this was her property.

"It's better than I had hoped. I can see it all." He swept his hand from one side of the cart to the other. "People relaxing, enjoying activities, swimming in the pool, taking trail rides, and of course, all the cabins will need to be upgraded with all the amenities."

"But aren't people coming to a ranch to kick back and experience real life on a working ranch?"

"Yes, but they want the luxury that is better than their homes. And I plan on delivering." He grinned and she couldn't wait until he was back in his car and all that was left of him was his taillights shining through little puffs of dust.

She pulled up next to his car and turned the cart off. She'd pop in and see if there were any of Quinn's cookies left and grab an apple for Bowie before going back to her office.

He turned on the seat. "So are you ready to sign?"

Man, he was pushy, but his enthusiasm reinforced her budding ideas. She could do something on a smaller scale to increase the viability of her ranch.

"Lucas, I'm sure you understand being an astute businessman. I need time to read your proposal, look over the numbers, and consult with my attorney. What kind of businessperson would I be if I didn't put in the work to evaluate everything? There is also the matter of my people to consider."

"We'd keep the majority on since we'll still have horses and cattle to tend and maybe some will even want to handle trail rides and fishing adventures." His eyes couldn't get any wider or brighter.

She put her hand out. "I'll be in touch in a few weeks and please don't think by calling, you can pressure me into making a quicker decision."

"Of course, Annie. Take all the time you need." He got out of the cart. "But I need an answer in four weeks. If we can't come to terms, I'll have to look elsewhere."

She nodded. She still wasn't going to answer him. The information he had given her might prove to be gold and why squander the opportunity?

"I promise I will be in touch with my decision in four weeks' time."

His head bobbed like it might pop off his neck. "I'll look forward to it and of course, it goes without saying, if you have any questions, any at all, you know how to find me."

"I have your number." In more ways than one. She gave him a bland smile. "Safe travels."

With one final brief handshake, he got in his car. Annie continued to sit on the golf cart until he was partway down the drive. Only then did she notice Linc lingering on the front porch. It was obvious by the scowl on his face that he had overheard the entire conversation.

"So that's it?" he said.

"It is. He salivated over each blade of grass. In a way it was fun to see the ranch through his eyes." She walked up the steps. "I'm going to see if I can pilfer a cookie and an apple from Quinn and head down to see Bowie. Want to come?"

He put his sunglasses on and stood up. "I have work to do."

She watched as he stalked off the porch, but what she couldn't understand was why the heck he kept making statements and walking away from her. What had she done except out of courtesy heard the man out and gotten a little free intel in the process?

She didn't have time to worry about what was stuck in Linc Cooper's craw. If she didn't get a move on, she'd be burning the midnight oil in her office because she sure as heck wasn't missing out on spending time with her babies.

. . .

Over dinner Annie told Mary what had happened with Lucas Gasperini.

"The information he gave me is detailed and I'm pretty confident I could start with a handful of cabins and offer a working ranch experience."

"That's a little out of our comfort zone. Don't you think you should focus on the garden and greenhouse before you take on a huge project like that?"

She was surprised Mary wasn't as enthusiastic as she was. This could be good for all of them, especially if she could get people to come out in the winter months. There was still a lot to do even then on a ranch; snow-based activities during the day and fireside at night. It was more low-key but winter was a very special time in Montana. She could figure out the specifics later, but the germ of the idea was niggling at her.

"Mary, I need to think about the long-term future for us all. Yeah, we've got cattle, but we've also got the river, and you and I have both fished there. The trout are amazing. What if we have a bad season and our crops dry up? How do I feed the livestock and all the ranch hands? An income from a small resort operation could be key. And I'm not thinking of making this a full-fledged enterprise. We'll always be a working ranch but with the added income of vacation rentals."

"It's not something Pops would like to have seen. He turned down Mr. Gasperini."

"No, he liked the idea of growing the ranch, but he'd never sell out. There's a difference." She could hear the sharpness in her voice and wasn't going to back down either.

Mary frowned. "Child, this is something you need to think long and hard about before you make any rash decisions. Once you start down that path and put good money into it, well, it's not as easy to undo."

She patted Mary's hand. "Don't worry. I'm not an impulsive little girl anymore. My job is to analyze facts and figures and I intend to spend the next few weeks taking a deeper dive into everything."

She got up from the table and picked up their plates. "I think Pops would be happy I was thinking outside the fences, looking to the future."

"He'd be happy if you were thinking about the future in a different way too. What's going on with you and Linc?"

She put the dishes in the sink and turned on the hot water. She liked to hand-wash them when she was mulling over an issue. "Nothing. He got really weird today and stormed off. I don't have time for that nonsense, and if you're talking about me having kids, I have plenty of time."

"You're approaching forty." Mary wagged her finger in her direction. "And I'd like to meet at least one of your babies before I walk through the pearly gates."

Annie leaned against the counter. "Let's get one thing straight. You're not going anywhere anytime soon because I need you with me, and when the time is right, I'll be happy to put a baby of mine in your arms. But I'm not rushing into anything until I have a man as fine as my dad or Pops in my life."

Her eyes grew misty. "Annie, open your eyes. You already do but the two of you need to talk and work a few things out."

She crossed the room and hugged Mary. "A

conversation requires two people and I'm not chasing down anyone to have a conversation." She kissed the soft wrinkled skin of Mary's cheek. "I love you, but please don't push. If Linc and I are meant to see what might be left between us, then we'll figure it out."

Annie couldn't help but wonder what Linc's problem was. She thought they had come so far in the last few weeks, but after today she wasn't so sure.

Chapter Twelve

Linc paced his small office. He'd left Annie standing on the porch after he refused to spend time with her. Why would he want to do that and get his hopes up? She was selling her legacy and their future and there wasn't a thing he could do about it. He stopped mid-stride. It didn't make any sense. She was so happy that Bowie had a colt, and she said he was the future of Grace Star's breeding program; that's if she still wanted to go in that direction instead of selling out to an arrogant resort developer. He tossed a pad across the room and it smacked against the wall. He had work to do but nothing good was going to come of him doing paperwork. He stashed his cell in his shirt pocket, the walkie-talkie in the holder on his belt, and grabbed his cowboy hat and strode out the door.

He rode fast and hard as if demons themselves were chasing him, but it didn't matter how hard he drove his horse. He couldn't forget the look on Annie's face when he left her standing on the porch. He eased Darby to a slow trot and patted his neck. "Good boy." He pulled him up short. Sitting tall in the saddle, he took in the distant mountains. The peace that washed over him made him wonder if he could change Annie's mind if he brought her out here. Maybe they could talk about why she had decided to sell the ranch to that lowlife. But Linc was just a ranch hand and she owned all that the eye could see.

He might be old-fashioned in his thinking, but his heart ached for what would be lost. Everything Pops had worked his entire life to achieve would be gone. Developers never stopped with just adding in a few cottages. Sure, they'd keep some cattle to add flavor to the experience, but Linc had heard about this happening in other areas. Within a few years, the working part of the ranch would evaporate like a summer rain on a hot day in the midst of a drought. Just as the land greedily absorbed the water, the tourists would suck dry what this ranch was meant to be.

Turning in his saddle, he looked in the direction of the river. The spring thaw had long since receded. Fishing was something he loved doing on his rare weekends off. He flicked the reins and Darby turned, plodding along at a comfortable pace. Now neither man nor horse were in any hurry to get anywhere.

A crackle came over the walkie.

"Linc, where are you? Over."

It was Clint and it was unusual for him to track Linc down. There was an understanding that when he took Darby out in the middle of the day, he needed to clear his head. His concern increased.

"I'm out in the south pasture. Over."

Clint said, "We've got a man down. Over."

"Location and who?" He didn't bother with

the over, but he did wait for the details before moving. It was never a good sign when he got called about an injury; that meant it was pretty serious.

"Jed, main barn. He got stepped on by a bull and I'm pretty sure his foot is gonna need attention, maybe surgery." He liked that Clint didn't waste words just for the sake of talking. It might not always be the cowboy way, but it was his way.

"Alert urgent care you're bringing him in and don't wait for me. I'm at least a couple miles away and thirty to forty minutes out. But keep in touch." He was ticked he had pushed Darby so hard on the way out, but Linc had to think of his mount's well-being and take it easier on the way in. Jed was in good hands with Clint, but ultimately every person and animal on this ranch was his responsibility.

"You got it, boss." As an afterthought, he said, "Over."

Linc nudged his spurs into Darby's sides and the quarter horse took off like a shot at a gallop until he was reined back to a steady cantor. He thought of Jed, a good man and hard worker. He wasn't one to take rest or needed recovery well. There would need to be jobs Jed could do while laid up but what they were was anyone's guess. Hopefully between now and when he got back from urgent care, Linc would have some idea. And of course, once Clint called, he'd have to go up to the house and fill Annie in on all the details. This would be a workmen's comp case and there was paperwork to be filled out.

The sun was low in the sky when Linc crossed to the main house. He was ready to bring Annie up to date on Jed's condition and maybe they'd even be able to talk about the developer too. The back door was ajar and Linc pushed it open and strode in. He didn't give it another thought that he should knock since he'd been walking into this house for over fifteen years. The lingering smell of dinner made his mouth water, and his gut knocking against his spine reminded him he needed to get some dinner after this.

"Annie?" He didn't want to go too far into

the house since she might be down the hall in her bedroom and that space was off-limits.

Muffled footsteps grew closer. Mary came around the door and stopped short.

"Linc, this is a surprise. Is everything alright?"

It was rare he came to the house after dinner unless Pops and he had business to discuss but even then, it had always been over a meal.

"Is Annie around? I need to talk to her." His heart skipped, wanting to be close to her and wishing he could take back the way he acted earlier.

Mary nodded and said she'd be right back.

A few minutes later Annie came into the kitchen, her hair wrapped in a towel on top of her head, wearing a faded pink bathrobe. He smothered a smile as he saw the wet trail of footprints she left behind her.

"What's up?"

He liked how she got right to the point. "Jed was taken to urgent care and now has been admitted to the hospital." She opened her mouth and he held up his hand. "Hold on. I'll give you all the details; just give me a second."

She pulled out a chair at the kitchen table. "Have a seat."

The wooden chair legs scraped over the floor and he sat, taking his hat off and resting it on his knee. The petal white of her throat caused his pulse to quicken while the soft smell of roses filled his senses. A bittersweet memory clouded his thinking—holding her in his arms and savoring the sweet floral scent. He pushed it aside and forced himself to stay focused on Jed's situation.

"A bull crushed Jed's foot earlier today. Clint took him to urgent care where they shipped him off to Bozeman for surgery to repair the broken bones and there's soft tissue damage too. Doc says he'll recover just fine, but he'll be out of commission for a while."

"Is anyone with him?"

Of course, her first concern would always be for one of her men. "Clint's there and he'll head back tomorrow. I was thinking of sending Rory down. You know as Jed begins to realize he has a long recovery ahead of him, well, it's not gonna be pretty."

"Good idea. Any time estimate of when he'll be released?"

He could see she was already thinking of Jed's recovery just as he had been since he learned of the surgery. "A few days, but less than a week."

"Is he in a cabin or a bunkhouse and what do we have in the way of helping him recover, and not just physically? If he's anything like every other cowboy on this ranch, I know sitting around is not his idea of a way to spend the day."

"He actually bunks with Rory in one of the newer cabins. But it's farther away from my office so it'd be hard for me to help out during the day."

She got up and poured them each a glass of water without asking if he wanted one. It was an old habit of hers to do something while she was trying to unravel a puzzle.

"What about in the dining hall? There are some rooms on the opposite side of the offices. We could fix one up to make it easy for Jed to get around and have company as he can tolerate it. In the event he needs something, there are people coming and going all the time." She sipped the water. "With the lounge right there and the other comforts of his own space, it might be the best solution until he can get back to his cabin."

Her heart was as big as the sky. She was so much like Pops, a younger, female version of his mentor and old friend.

"That would work. I'll see who I can tap to get it ready."

She shook her head. "Everyone's busy this time of year; it's not like we're up to our backsides in snow where guys are looking for things to do to pass the time. I'll come down and Mary can lend a hand. If we need heavy lifting, I'll let you know."

His admiration for her grew. She wasn't going to sit in the office and make suggestions; she was rolling up her sleeves to make it happen.

She held up her finger. "But I want you to keep me up to date on his progress. When it's time for him to come back to the ranch, I'll pick him up."

"You might need some muscle so I'll go with you if you'd like." He stopped short. "You're not going to pick him up in your car, are you?"

With a snort, she laughed. "Hardly. I was going to take the dually. The quad cab has plenty of room and he should be comfortable in the back."

"Good choice."

She sat back down. "How's the bull? Did he get hurt at all?"

This woman never ceased to amaze him, always thinking of every aspect of a situation.

"He's a tough old dude, been around the block and not even a scuff on his hide."

She grinned. "Good to know." She placed her hand on his arm and it warmed under her touch. He placed his hand over hers. Would the intimacy of the moment be the opening he needed to talk about this afternoon?

She blinked and pulled her hand away. "Um, did I tell you Daphne is coming out for a visit?"

His face blanked, the moment lost. "Daphne?"

"You remember, I talked about her earlier, short, red hair, and a few freckles for extra flair."

"Ah, yeah." They were definitely not going to talk about earlier and he wanted nothing more than to clear the air between them. He even wanted to revisit what happened when she was twenty-one. If he had it to do over again, he never would have pushed her away.

"She wants to come out for a couple of weeks. So, I was thinking when I go to Boston, I might just have her take a trip back with me. She's not a good flyer."

His heart sank. She was leaving and going to Boston. He pushed back his chair and set his hat back on his head. His mouth was dry and his gut felt as if he'd been sucker punched.

"It'll be fun for both of you." He touched the rim of his hat and gave her a slight nod. "I'll let you know about Jed tomorrow. Have a good night."

His boots clicked against the floor as he walked out, the door banging shut behind him. Why did he keep thinking they could get off the trail they were on and find their way back to each other? He was a fool to think he'd ever be enough to keep her happy here. Annie had a life in Boston, full of all the things the city could offer her. What was there here? Cows, horses, and wide-open spaces. He walked down the path in the growing darkness. Once he was in the shadow of a barn, he turned and looked back at the house. Lights were being clicked on room by room. He guessed Annie was working her way back to her bedroom. She never did like the darkness, except when they were sitting in the back of his pickup truck under the stars.

He took a step in the direction of the house, but then halted. She needed to figure out what she wanted out of life, and if that meant he had to move on and start over, he would. But there was one thing he'd do before that happened. He was going to tell Annie Grace that he had always loved her and would until the day he took his last breath. Maybe there was still hope for them and if she wanted to live in Boston and he was lucky enough that she'd want him to be by her side, well, maybe he could find a way to make it work. Their memories kept him on the ranch, and he savored those occasional visits when she came home to see her grandfather. Those fleeting moments were better than nothing and he knew all too well that a life without Annie was half a life.

He hurried back to his office. There was time to scope out which room would work best for

Jed's recovery, and tomorrow there were mountains to move to make sure they were ready. Neither Annie nor Linc would accept anything less. At least there they would always be on the same page.

Chapter Thirteen

Annie had taken one last look at Jed's temporary bunk room. He was coming back to the ranch tomorrow. She was driving to Bozeman to pick him up, and Clint was going with her. Linc had a lot to get done, but if she was being real with herself, it wasn't that he couldn't be spared from the ranch; it was more how she would spend a few hours with him, alone. All her simmering emotions might not be able to be reined in.

Now back in her office, she smothered a laugh, not that there was anyone in there to hear her. What would he think if she flung her arms around his neck and pulled him in for a smoking hot kiss? She ran a finger across her lower lip. It would satisfy one lingering question she had. Had he gotten better with age? That kiss on the front steps hadn't done anything to answer the question but really had left her with more. She hadn't had any complaints over her ability to kiss, but then again, the only man who ever lit her fire was the one man who crushed her, and her heart had never recovered. Or was it more than that?

Once when she had asked Pops why he never got married after Pippa died, he told her that sometimes you're lucky enough to find your one great love and no one else could ever walk beside you in life. Even though he had dated after a while, he hadn't bothered with anything long term; Pippa had his heart for all eternity. Could Linc have been her one great love and now she'd have to settle for second best if she wanted to have kids?

Mary tapped on the door casing. "Annie, do you have a minute?"

She smiled at the older woman. "Of course. I was lost in thought." While Mary sat down in the leather chair in her office, Annie wondered why she had never married all those years ago. "Since you're here, can I ask you a question about love?"

Mary sat back and crossed her legs, her hands folded demurely in her lap. "Child, I'm an open book; ask away."

"I know your husband died when you were a young woman and you came to live at the ranch shortly after that, but why didn't you ever re-marry? Didn't you ever want to have a family of your own?"

Her eyes grew misty. "There was a time when I thought I was going to have children and Pippa and I would raise our families together. When Jay died in the flash flood, I was so young and I couldn't imagine how I was going to sur-vive, but your grandmother, rest her soul, wouldn't hear of me living by myself in town. I was only twenty-five at the time; what did I know about life? And I'd just buried my hus-band. We both thought it would be a few weeks, but it turned into months and even when I was asked out on a date, it just didn't feel right." She placed a hand over her heart. "Jay wouldn't want me pining for him but the future I dreamed of died with him."

Annie opened her mouth and the words evaporated from her lips as Mary shook her head. "No. Don't go feelin' sorry for me. Sometimes life gives you a different path and you need to walk down it. The ranch was growing like wildfire and your grandmother had her hands full with your daddy. He was always gettin' into mischief. At that time, I was helping Buck cook for the ranch hands and basically working at whatever needed to get done and I was happy. Why change what didn't need changin'."

"Was Jay the love of your life?"

Her eyes sparkled and a small smile played over her lips. "I guess you could say that. Do I wish we had more time together, sure, but I wouldn't trade what we did have for a different life."

"Mary, I'm sorry you lost him. I bet Jay was a great man."

"He was, much like your Linc." Her smile widened while she shifted in her chair. "What are you going to do about that situation?"

"Nothing. He's made it pretty clear we're old friends and he works for me." She looked away so Mary wouldn't see the hurt in her eyes. She didn't need a mirror to tell her she couldn't hide how she felt about him.

"You know, Annie, the one thing about life is that it's always changing. It's like the river after the spring floods. You know it will always be flowing, but underneath the surface the bed has changed; new deep pockets of fishing holes are waitin' to be discovered. But if you don't drop a line, you'll never even know what you could land."

"Are you comparing Linc to a fish?" Her heart felt a little lighter which was typical when Mary started making up her own analogies for life. "And we've both been fishing and came up empty."

"But did you? We're still talking about the two of you for over fifteen years. Which means something's on your line. You might want to reel it in before it slips away and this time forever."

Annie got up and walked to the window. In the distance she could see some of her men on horses, herding the cows back to the barn. A storm was brewing and who knew what would happen if there was a flash flood. It was better to keep the herd all together. Was Linc working the herd too? There was no way she could tell one rider from another at this distance; they were all just moving blots.

Leaning against the windowsill, she looked at Mary. "You didn't come in to talk about the ancient past and I derailed the conversation, so what's up?"

She took a deep breath and exhaled. "I'm thinking it's time to retire. I was thinking the end of the summer season and I'd move before winter."

Annie's heart dropped. Was she ill or worse? Sinking into her office chair, she asked, "Mary, are you okay? Is there anything I should know?"

She leaned across the desk and patted Annie's clasped hands. "I'm healthy as a horse but I am slowing down and it's harder than it used to be to keep the house spotless, garden, and cook." With a hitch in her voice, she said, "So if I retired, I could move to one of the communities for old folks and live out my golden years."

Stunned didn't begin to describe how Annie felt. It was a good thing she sat down or her legs wouldn't have kept her upright.

With a vigorous shake of her head, Annie said, "Nope, you're not moving anywhere. This is your home and it's where you'll stay."

"But I can't keep up and you deserve to have your home's standards maintained just as I've done for many years."

She got up from the desk and dropped down beside Mary's chair. Taking the older woman's wrinkled hands, she said, "Let's get one thing clear. You are not moving anywhere. You're my family and I need you here with me. Call it selfish but I couldn't bear it if I didn't get to see you across the breakfast table every morning or hear you sing off-key when you're fixing a pot of coffee."

Mary's cheeks flashed a deep shade of pink. "You're a sweet girl and it means a great deal that you want me to stay. But I can't keep up with the house."

"Then I'll hire someone, or two someones, to come in and clean or do whatever needs to be done and you can supervise them, just like you're doing with Polly. When I'm not here, you can be my ears and eyes."

Mary tipped her head to one side. "What do you mean, when you're not here? Where are you going?"

She smiled and her voice became less pleading. "I have to go back to Boston, pack up my storage unit, and move the rest of my stuff here. I can't very well live in Montana if my favorite books and winter clothes are in another state."

"So, you're leaving your job at the firm to run the ranch full-time?" It was like a light bulb just brightened her face.

"Now, don't go telling everyone what I'm up to yet, but I've been reading the papers that our friend, Mr. Gasperini, left, you know about building a resort. He wants to destroy what's here and just use the framework to bring people in, but there's merit to the idea of having guest cottages. However, instead of it being for show, we'll still have a working ranch and a resort experience." When I come home, I'm bringing Daphne with me and I'm going to propose she run the place.

She has experience running events, and this would be like a never-ending event."

Mary pulled her into a fierce hug and let her go just as fast, then placed a hand against her cheek. "Pops would be proud to know you're gonna make your mark here. What did Linc say?"

She rocked back on her heels and stood up. "I haven't told him yet. He was a jerk the other day when I met with Mr. Gasperini and since he didn't seem interested, I didn't share my plans. He can stew for a while." She pursed her lips. "And you've been sworn to secrecy. If Linc comes poking around while I'm gone, your lips are sealed with superglue."

"That sounds a might uncomfortable, but you've got my word. He won't hear anything from me."

"Good. Now, while I'm gone, why don't you start spreading the word that we're looking for a housekeeper and a cook, because trust me"—she laughed—"the stove and I are not friends and takeout isn't an option this far out of town."

Mary clapped her hands together with a hoot. "I'm not giving up my kitchen duty, so don't worry about feeding me charred food. But help with the housework and a few other things would be good. Maybe this person will help in your new cottages too. It might even work into a full-time job for the right person."

Annie pulled Mary into her arms again and she kissed the petal softness of her cheek. She smelled faintly of roses and lemon polish. "You know you're like a second grandmother to me and you're not living in some old folks apartment any-where. I've spent too many years away from my home and you. It's time we make up for those lost years."

Mary looked her in the eyes. "I'm not the only one who needs to make up lost time with you. Bait your hook and see who might nibble on it." A gleam shone in her eye. "I'd like to be an hon-orary great-grandmother someday."

With a chuckle and a grin, Annie said, "Stop pushing, Mary, or I'll rethink that retirement vil-lage in Phoenix."

She waved her hand. "Nah, I'd only go as far as town."

"The only place you're going is to the kitchen.

With picking up Jed, I need road trip cookies, oatmeal with chocolate chips and nuts, please."

She paused in the doorway. "Is Linc going with you?"

Annie exhaled a deep sigh. Mary just wasn't going to let up on her and Linc being together or at least trying to work out their past. It was something she'd think about on the trip back to Boston but for now she needed to wrap things up here, get Jed, and then tomorrow she'd hop a plane and be at Daphne's place tomorrow night. If nothing else, it would be good to see her.

"How about we agree that I'll think about what you said and you let me have time and space to make this decision."

Mary beamed. "That's all I ask. There's a reason no one else ever stuck for either of you."

After she left the room, Annie doublechecked her travel arrangements for tomorrow. She'd drive to the airport, and then when she and Daphne returned, no one would have to pick them up. The sounds of off-key singing drifted to her and the smell of baking cookies made her smile. With one final look at her computer, she powered down, packed her travel bag, and went in search of the one sweet treat Mary had always made just for her.

Jed was settled as best he could be in his room and Annie was on her way through the lounge when Linc came in. He smiled but it didn't reach his eyes. It was obvious he was still annoyed with her.

"Hey, Linc." She pointed down the hall. "Jed seems happy to be out of the hospital, although he said he could do without all the special treatment."

"That's Jed for you. Always wanting to be in the saddle and in the background."

He took his hat off and ran his hand over his hair. He looked tired and in need of a break.

"I'm headed up to the house. Do you want to come up and have dinner with me? We can catch up on a few things before I go."

His brow furrowed. "Where are you going?"

"I'm flying out to Boston tomorrow." She couldn't read his facial expression as a mask dropped over it. What was his problem now? She shook her head. "If you can't, no big deal. I just thought we could take care of a few things, but we can catch up via email if you'd prefer."

"When are you coming back?" His voice was monotone and the smile that had been on his face faded.

"I'm not sure yet. But I'll let you know when I've made arrangements."

He half turned. "Tell Mary thanks for the dinner invite, but I've lost my appetite." He gave her a curt nod and turned on his heel, his boots thundering over the wooden floor as he strode toward his office.

"What the heck was that all about?" She was torn. Should she follow him and hash this out once and for all or just leave it and him alone? Linc's office door slamming made the decision for her. When was she going to learn that loving Linc cost her countless tears and more heartache and as much as she was tempted to try and see if they could find their way back to each other, it was a lost cause?

She closed the door on the dining hall softly and stepped out into the cool early evening air.

Goosebumps danced across her bare arms as she ran up to the house. At least Mary would be happy to have her company tonight. She took one final look over her shoulder, just in case Linc had followed her out, but he wasn't there so she walked away.

Chapter Fourteen

Annie had been gone three days and Linc's mood wasn't any better than the night she said she was leaving. He adjusted the bit on Darby and rubbed his velvety soft nose.

"Ready to get some work done today?" The gelding nickered softly as if agreeing they both needed to get outside and stretch their legs.

He swung into the saddle and headed toward the north pasture. He was going to ride the fence to see what needed to be repaired. In this mood it was best to be by himself. He rounded the side of the dining hall to check on Jed before he set off.

After he tied Darby up, he was taking the steps two at a time when he noticed a small gray pickup truck headed in his direction. As it grew closer, he saw a woman in the driver's seat. He paused before going inside, waiting to see who it was since he didn't recognize her or the truck.

The woman parked next to one of the ATVs in front of the building and got out. She waved a hand in greeting and flashed him a friendly smile.

"Hello, I'm Lauren Sullivan and I'm looking for Jed Steele." She scanned the area and climbed the steps, carrying a duffel bag over one shoulder and a laptop bag in the other hand. "I was told this would be the building, but now I'm not sure."

Ms. Sullivan was tall and thin, wearing a dark-blue track suit and bright-white sneakers. Her short dark hair was in a no-nonsense style and Linc noticed she wore minimal makeup.

"I'm Lincoln Cooper, the manager, and what exactly do you do?" He had a suspicion it had something to do with Jed's recovery, but people didn't make house calls anymore so how did she get here?

"Sorry." She adjusted the strap on the duffel bag and stuck out her hand. After giving his a firm shake, she said, "I'm the physical therapist that Annie Grace hired to work with Jed."

Well, this was certainly unexpected. When anyone needed rehab, there was a small office in town or Doc Harper, their local doctor, gave exercises to do and no one expected you to spend long hours trying to get better; you just did.

"Annie hired you when?" He could hear the bark in his voice but didn't really care. Why hadn't she told him so he could have gotten things ready for Jed? After all, these guys were his responsibility, and then he acquiesced; the men were ultimately her responsibility too.

"From the notes I got, it was set up when he was discharged, and Annie asked that I come to the ranch since he won't be able to drive for a few weeks."

He nodded. Annie didn't want to have anyone taking off from their job to make sure Jed got what he needed to fully recover. It was a double-edged sword. Either she thought he couldn't handle it or she was just being nice. But it was an interesting thought. Pops would never have brought someone out; he would have driven the person to town, making the thirty-plus-minute trip as many times as necessary. Annie had taken the easy way out since she wasn't even in the state to help out one of her own.

"Lincoln, is Jed inside?"

"It's just Linc and yeah, come on in. I'll show you where to find him." He took her duffel bag and pushed open the door, having Lauren walk in ahead of him. "I'll show you around first, and if you need anything, you can always find Quinn, our cook, in the kitchen." He pointed to a swinging wood door.

Leading the way down the hall, Linc pointed out the bathroom and another lounge area, then they came to Jed's room. He rapped on the door and waited until he heard, *come in*. He walked through the door first, unsure if Jed knew what was in store for him and if he was even decent.

"Jed, Annie set you up with a physical thera-pist and…"

"Yeah, I knew someone was coming out." He looked around Linc and gave Lauren a half smile.

"So, you're the lucky person who's going to torture me?" He heaved himself off the chair to a standing position and wobbled on his crutches.

She smiled and thanked Linc for showing her the way. He stepped into the hall and before he left, Jed said, "Let's get this program going. The sooner I can get around, the sooner I can get back to work."

He liked the determination he heard in Jed's voice. That was one tough cowboy.

It was a long, solitary day riding the fence line, but he knew the weak spots and made notes to pass to Rory to order the supplies. As he let Darby set the pace for the trip back to the ranch, his thoughts turned to Annie and hiring the therapist to come to the ranch. It had to be expensive and why would she do that especially when she planned on selling the place? If only he'd been able to talk to her before she left; maybe he could have changed her mind about the impending sale.

After another quarter of a mile or so, he took his hat off and wiped his brow with his shirtsleeve and that was when it dawned on him. She had invited him up to the house to talk. If he hadn't been such a stubborn mule, maybe there would have been time to sort this out and convince her not to return to Boston. Was he too late or might it be possible to stop the horse from throwing a shoe? That was a poor metaphor for what needed to be done. He took off at a gallop, in search of Mary. Hopefully she'd have some of the answers he needed.

Linc knocked on the kitchen door and strode inside. "Mary?"

The house was silent but there was a pitcher of tea brewing on the counter. He glanced out the kitchen window which overlooked her garden. He went out the back door and around the corner.

She looked his way. "I was wondering when you'd come around."

He furrowed his brow. "What do you mean? Do you need some help?" He picked up her woven basket overloaded with vegetables and what smelled like mint.

"No, I don't need any, but I think you might." She nodded to the house. "Come inside. I made some cookies and we'll have tea."

She walked ahead of him, and he noticed her gait was slightly unsteady. He reached out his hand to her and she grasped his arm. Throwing him a grateful smile, she said, "I've had a busy few days and I'm a little tired."

He ushered her inside and held out a chair at the kitchen table. "You relax and I'll take care of getting our snack." He gave her a worried glance as he poured two glasses of tea.

"Would you add some mint to our glasses? It will be refreshing. That's why I went out to the garden to begin with, and when I saw the tomatoes and cucumbers needed to be picked, I got carried away."

He set the glass in front of her and grabbed the cookie tin from the counter. She smiled her thanks and patted his hand.

"You're a good man, Linc."

"Are you feeling better?" He was satisfied her color was returning to normal and she looked better, but he'd reach out to Annie and let her know

Mary had been unsteady. If anything happened to her, he'd never forgive himself.

He withdrew a cookie from the tin and waited for her to get one before he said, "Are you sure you're feeling better?"

She dipped her head and didn't look him in the eye. His gut clenched. Did this mean he shouldn't leave her alone? Mary was like his favorite aunt and he'd do whatever was necessary to help her.

"I'm better and it's always good to see your handsome face in the middle of a workday. So, what brings you by?"

He set the cookie aside and leaned closer to her. "Why is Annie selling the ranch?"

She pulled back and her face scrunched up. "What makes you think she's selling the place? Did she say something to you before she flew out?"

"She invited me up to dinner and I blew her off. I was annoyed with her and wasn't in the mood to listen." Which had been just one of his stupid mistakes with her. "When she said she was going home, I shut down."

She actually made a *tsk, tsk* sound and shook her head. "Some things never change with you two. Just once I'd like you both to sit down and scale this mountain between you or get some dynamite and blow it up."

"I don't know what you're talking about." He leaned back in his chair and propped his leg across his knee. His heart thudded in his chest. Was Mary about to call him out? He deserved it and had no defense other than how he had lived his life was always for the best of others.

"You should be taking a hard look at your relationship with Annie. This push-pull between the two of you has to stop. It's not healthy for either of you."

He wanted to protest that he wasn't doing that. He had done his best to keep her out of his thoughts and heart, but it hadn't worked; even when he broke her heart, she remained in his.

She shook her finger at him. "I knew it. You've never stopped loving our Annie, but instead of telling her, you keep pickin' fights and pushin' her away. What are you scared of, actually living the life you deserve?"

"That's not it at all." He looked across the room. On the far wall there was a picture of Annie and Pops on horseback. It had to have been taken years ago; she still had braces and she was adorable, even then.

"Why don't you be honest with yourself. Pushing her away means you can do what, give her a different life that you decided was right for her?" Again, she shook her head. "You've wasted so many years making decisions you shouldn't be making and what has it done for Annie? Do you see her happily married with her own family?" Her voice ticked up a notch. "The way I see it, you need to make a decision. Either tell her you love her or that it's really over and find someone so that you're not available."

This conversation wasn't going the way he expected. Linc wanted to ask about the ranch and her plans and Mary had turned this around so it was about his relationship with Annie. She got up from the table, steady on her feet.

"I'd suggest you figure out what you want and after you do, decide what your role is here. You can have what you want. When she gets back, buck up and do us all a favor. Talk to Annie." She pointed to the door. "I'm tired and I have things to do."

He hesitated before standing, hearing her words that he needed to leave, but he was torn. He still hadn't gotten the answer for his burning question, was Annie selling out. The stern look on her face wasn't softening so for today there would be no answers. He'd known Mary most of his life. There wasn't any way to convince her to talk about it either. Maybe he'd take her advice and figure out what he wanted. He dropped a kiss on her cheek. "Call if you need anything."

She gave him a firm pat on the cheek. "I love you but what I need is for you to make a final decision."

He gave her a fast hug. Her body felt small and frail in his arms and suddenly he was reminded life was finite. "I love you too."

He left the house and headed in the direction of the horse barn. When all else failed, being around the animals was a balm to his soul. He needed to check on Bowie and Beau, and with them, he'd feel closer to Annie.

. . .

Later that night Linc lay reclined on his sofa, nursing a beer and thinking about his conversation with Mary. It was less than a conversation and more of a one-sided scolding. He had to grin; she treated him like he was the gawky teen trailing after Annie during summer breaks from high school and then college. Had he ever thought of moving past his feelings for her and building a life or were they more like a pair of eagles and they bonded at first sight? Could he live the rest of his life without ever seeing her again or worse knowing she had found love with another man? So many questions had no answers until he talked to her.

He sat up on the couch and flipped open the chest he used for a coffee table. He withdrew a framed photo of him and Annie when she had graduated from high school. She hadn't changed much; she'd just gotten more beautiful with shorter hair. He set it on the side table and wondered why he had pushed her away. Was it fear that she'd leave him and break his heart? He smacked his forehead with the back of his hand; he was a first-class idiot. He grabbed his cell and punched the speed dial button.

On the fourth ring, he heard her breathless hello.

"Annie, it's me, Linc."

He heard her suck in a breath, and then she said, "Hey. This is unexpected. Is everything okay?"

With a sinking feeling in the pit of his stomach, he wondered if that meant she wasn't happy to hear from him. *What the heck*. He said, "I, um, wanted to let you know I was up at the house today and Mary seemed a little unsteady on her feet. We had some tea and I stayed for a while, just to make sure she was okay, but I thought you'd want to know."

"Oh, she hasn't said anything."

Her words were laced with concern. He wanted her to know but he hadn't meant to drop it on her like this without any lead-up. With her being so far away, that was a good way to cause her to worry even more. He wanted to reassure her. "I'll keep an eye on her and make sure she's okay, but I wanted to give you a heads-up."

"I appreciate the call."

He didn't want to hang up—not yet. "The new physical therapist started working with Jed and it was real nice of you to have her come to the ranch."

"It just made sense to keep it simple and if Jed wasn't out riding around, he'd have a better chance to recover more quickly."

"Good idea." He wasn't sure what else to say. Silence hung between them.

"Well, if there's nothing else, I'll see you at some point."

What had she said? "You're coming back to the ranch?" He held his breath.

"Yes, I have a lot to take care of in a short time span."

He felt the sucker punch to his midsection. "Safe travels."

Chapter Fifteen

It had been three weeks since Annie flew out to Boston and now, she and Daphne sailed through the gate in Bozeman and onto the concourse on their way to baggage claim. The flight from Boston had been smooth and even better, on time. She couldn't wait to get back to the ranch, eat Mary's home cooking, and the best part, see how Beau was growing. He was already a month old, and he certainly was going to be a handsome boy. She had hopes he'd be the stud to start her extension to a horse farm; it was part of her diversification plan. And the guests would need mounts too.

"Earth to Annie." Daphne poked her arm. "I forgot how beautiful this airport is with the towering stone supports and all this post and beam architecture. It is a great way to start my vacation." She twirled around and pulled her hat off to toss it in the air, but then looked around at the security guards and put it back on her head. "Probably not the best idea to have a Mary Tyler Moore moment inside the airport."

Annie's heart was light and full at the same time. Now that she was back in Montana, this felt right; she was home. Even though Pops had done an amazing job with the ranch for years, she was going to start making changes, some slow and some not so slow, and make her mark. But the one dark cloud hanging over her new life was Linc. Could they resolve their issues and find their way back to each other? After being apart, she knew that was one of the most important things she wanted to be happy here.

"Yeah, skip the tossing of your hat. We'll go for a ride tomorrow and you can do it then." She glanced at Daphne who already looked more relaxed. This place had a way of doing that to a person. "After we get our bags, I'm going to give Mary a call and let her know we'll stop in town to grab a bite so she doesn't need to start cooking tonight."

They stepped onto the escalator and arrived in baggage claim. A cluster of people Annie recognized from their flight were hanging around an empty carousel. She withdrew her phone. "Will you watch for our bags?"

With a wave of her hand, Daphne stepped closer to the belt. "Take your time."

"Hey, Mary." She answered on the fourth ring which wasn't surprising since house phones weren't in every room and she always put the handsets back in their cradles.

"Annie, are you on the ground?"

With a small laugh, she said, "Yes, we're in Bozeman, waiting for our bags." It was cute that Mary always asked if she was on the ground, not really wanting to understand she wouldn't call from the plane. "I wanted to let you know we'll stop in River Junction and grab dinner. Do you want me to bring you a piece of pie? I was thinking of stopping at the Filler Up Diner. I'm sure Maggie's got a few flavors to choose from."

"No need to stop. I've already made chili and corn bread." Half a beat later, she said, "But if you wanted to stop and pick up a huckleberry pie, I wouldn't say no to a sliver."

Annie laughed loudly but through the din of the room, no one took notice. "I can do that. We'll see you soon and I'm looking forward to a big hug."

"Child, you've been missed around here and not just by me."

But had Linc missed her at all or was it like all the other times she'd left? Just an, *I'll catch up with you next time you're back.* "I missed you too."

"Drive safe and tell Daphne her room is all ready for her to stay for a nice long visit."

Annie glanced over as Daphne pulled two large suitcases off the belt before they got by her. "I'll let you tell her. I gotta run but see you soon."

She grabbed the two other bags that slipped by Daphne. "So, chick, I think we're ready to get the car and hit the road." She looked at the bags and thought of her car. It wasn't exactly made for all this luggage, but they'd make it work. Even if she had to take clothes out of the larger suitcase and stuff the smaller one inside it, all that mattered was there was no place like home in Montana.

Annie pulled under the portico in front of the house and before she could turn off the car, the front door opened and Mary was rushing down the stone steps. The smile on her face couldn't be any wider. It was almost as good as a warm hug and she was glad that some things never changed. Annie pushed open the car door and met her at the bottom with her arms wide. It had felt like she'd been gone years, not weeks.

"Mary." She held her tight. "Wow, it's so good to see you."

She cupped her cheek with her hand and said, "It's good to get away but better to come home." She held out her arm for Daphne to join their hug.

"Welcome back to the ranch, Daph. It's been much too long since you've been here for fun."

Mary kissed her cheek and with a twinkle in her eye, she asked, "Did you get pie?"

"Old woman, you're incorrigible. Not only did I get pie, but I also picked up six cupcakes. Maggie used some stout from The Lucky Bucket and said we had to try them and let her know what we think."

Mary clasped her hands together. "Beer in cake, I can't wait."

Annie and Daphne unloaded the car with Mary overseeing the operation, holding the box of pie and cake. "How on earth did you get all that in your little car?"

"It wasn't easy, but I was highly motivated." Annie closed the trunk and picked up the last two bags. "And for the record, I have a moving truck that will make a delivery in a couple of weeks with the rest of my *can't live without it* stuff."

"'Bout time is all I can say. Now, come inside; you must be starving."

She closed the door after the ladies got inside. Annie kicked off her clogs, flinging them to the corner of the entrance hall, and suggested Daphne do the same.

"What's been going on around here?" She hoped her question sounded casual and not like she was asking about a certain dark-haired cowboy.

"We'll talk over dinner. Do you girls want to use the washroom first?"

Daphne asked, "Which bedroom is mine?"

Mary took her handbag from her shoulder. "I'll help you." She gave a pointed look at Annie. "Take a minute to catch your breath. You're looking a bit flushed."

Of course she was; it was her natural reaction when she started thinking about Linc. She slung the two carry-on bags over her shoulders and pushed the two roller bags down the hall to her room. Mary needed to stop reading her thoughts. Or she needed to stop thinking of Linc. She suppressed a grin. What fun would that be if Mary wasn't sticking her nose into her love life?

The smell of chili lured her to the kitchen, and by the time she got there, Daphne and Mary were chattering like magpies on a fence. When Daphne had come for the funeral, it had been a quick trip, basically in one day for the service and out the next. Before that it had been a couple of years since she had the time to visit. But just having her at the ranch had been a balm to Annie's sadness during the funeral. Tomorrow Annie was going to talk to her about the resort plans and how Daphne was an important part of the future. Heck, she'd even build her a cabin on the property if that's what it took.

She leaned against the wall outside the kitchen, unseen, and listened to the two most important women in her life. Yes, she wanted to do it all, but before she started spending money like wildfire, she'd better work on the budget and be responsible. She couldn't spend money that she needed to maintain the cattle operation. She'd need to tap into her own funds and her inheritance from her parents to make the resort a reality. Until then, the main house had more than enough rooms for Daphne and a few more people. Pops had wanted the house to be comfortable for anyone she brought home, so he added on a second floor with a couple of guest suites and that's where Daphne was going to be staying.

She went around the corner and smiled. No sense letting on that there was anything weighing on her mind tonight. "Something sure does smell good."

"You're just in time. I was about to dish up dinner." Mary pointed to the refrigerator. "I'm not sure what you want to drink, but I did get some of that white wine you like or there's beer and of course lemonade and iced tea."

Daphne's eyes lit up. "Wine? Yes, please."

"Shall I make it three glasses?" She waited while Mary decided. It was rare she had a glass of wine, but there were special occasions when she would indulge.

"Yes, let's celebrate. After all, tonight is the beginning of a new future at Grace Star and that deserves a toast."

Annie poured three glasses while Daphne placed the breadbasket and serving bowl of steaming hot chili on the breakfast nook table. Mary crossed the room and Annie noticed that she was walking markedly slower than when she left. Before she got to the chair, she seemed to waver and grabbed the table. In a few quick steps, she slipped an arm around Mary's waist to steady her.

"What's going on? You seem like something's bothering your right leg and were just dizzy."

"It just gets a little numb occasionally but nothing for you to worry about, and I'm a little tired."

Now that sent a cold finger of fear up Annie's spine. Whenever Mary said there was nothing to worry about, that was the time to start.

"Have you called the doc?" She pulled out the chair for Mary to sit down. Daphne was watching them to see what might happen next.

"No need. It's just the old age monster stalking me."

Annie waited until Mary looked into her wide eyes and she didn't blink. She could not lose Mary, not yet. "We're going to call Doc Harper tomorrow and have him check you out." Mary started to protest but Annie shook her head. "This isn't a discussion of if you should or shouldn't. Linc called me while I was gone and mentioned that you were unsteady."

Mary pursed her lips. "He shouldn't have done that."

"I'm glad he did and I'm even more glad that I'm home and can take you into town for the appointment myself." She wasn't trusting Mary's health to just anyone and if Doc didn't have answers, she'd get her an appointment in Bozeman. She blinked away the tears that hovered on her lashes. There was a catch in her voice when she said, "Please, do this for me? I couldn't bear to have anything happen to you." She knew there was an almost desperate tone to her voice but she didn't care. Mary was the last link to her family; there wasn't anyone else who knew her parents. That day would come but she prayed it wouldn't be soon.

Mary patted her arm. "If you insist, I'll go, but I won't be happy about it."

Annie threw her arms around Mary and held her close. She whispered, "Thank you." Clearing her throat, she said, "Now about this chili, is there shredded cheese and sour cream in the refrigerator?"

"Of course. I know how you like it and it might be a bit spicier tonight so you might need an extra dollop."

Daphne slipped into the kitchen area, leaving them alone. Annie rested her forehead against Mary's. "Please take care of your health. I can't bear to lose you too."

"Child, I don't plan on riding through the pearly gates anytime soon. I've got way too much to do to get your resort off the ground to be thinking of dying. But at some point, when I leave this earth, you're gonna be just fine." She tipped Annie's chin up. "But you need to do something for me."

"Anything. Name it." Her heart thudded, knowing she'd walk over hot coals for Mary.

"Sit down with Linc and talk things out. Your feelings for him are as deep and true as they were all those years ago. I've never been one to talk much about soulmates, but I know when the connection is unbreakable between two people and that's what you have with Linc."

With a shake of her head, she said, "He's spent years pushing me away. Nothing has changed." But Mary was right; she loved Linc and that wasn't different. It had only taken one sweet, unforgettable kiss when she was seventeen to surrender her heart to him. Even though their relationship hadn't gone as she'd hoped, she wouldn't change a thing. Annie knew she longed to talk to Linc. Finally, she said, "I'll think about it but you're still going to the doctor."

Daphne hovered in the doorway and Annie waved her back in. The tension in the room relaxed since Annie and Mary had each gotten what they wanted. Daphne sat down and picked up her wineglass.

"I'd like to make a toast." She waited for Annie and Mary to lift their glasses. "To our futures and whatever that may be, but let's plan on spending more time together."

They tapped glasses and Mary glanced at Annie. She cocked a brow and Annie smiled. Tomorrow was going to be life-changing in many ways. Mary would see the doctor; she'd offer Daphne a new job, and finally she'd figure out what she wanted to say to Linc. Would she shoot straight and tell him how she felt or just keep their relationship strictly business and find a way to tell him they had to release each other from this invisible lasso between them?

Annie's head hurt just thinking of not having a future with him and she didn't want to think about Linc spending his life with another woman. She glanced at Mary who tipped her head to the side and winked. Well, the sneaky little devil, Mary's not-so-subtle pushes to get her to talk to Linc was exactly what she had decided to do and it wasn't going to be about the future of Grace Star Ranch. It was going to be much more personal.

She held up her glass. "Mary, you win."

"No, child, you will."

Chapter Sixteen

Linc sat on his porch in the growing darkness. Annie's car was parked in front of the main house and it eased his mind to know she was home. Tomorrow he was going to find her and they were going to work out their issues. He knew in his heart his deception had gone on long enough and he couldn't continue working for her if she didn't know the truth; he had never stopped loving her. If, after he laid his heart on the line, she wanted him to leave, he would go and never look back. For the first time in two weeks he was content. Knowing she was close by, even if it was only temporary, was enough for him.

After the darkness wrapped around him like a comfortable old blanket, he went inside but not before looking at the main house as the outside light was extinguished. Had it been an invitation for him to come up?

The following morning Linc made a small pot of coffee at his place. He didn't want to go to the dining hall and mingle with his men. Everyone knew what needed to get done and the last thing they needed was to be micromanaged. He heard the old grandfather clock clang eight times. For ranch life that was almost midmorning, but he wanted to be respectful. Annie was more than likely tired from traveling. A sharp rap on his door caught him by surprise.

He swung open the door and his breath was sucked from his lungs. Standing on the porch in a black tee, well-worn jeans, and scuffed black cowboy boots was Annie.

"Morning." She strode through the open door and headed toward the kitchen. "Mind if I help myself to coffee?"

What the heck was she doing here? He was going up to the house to talk to her; this wasn't part of his plan. Stunned didn't begin to cover seeing her in his cabin.

She pointed at the door. "Might want to close it and keep the bugs out."

He closed the door with a *thud*, but his boots were nailed to the floor. "I, um, I didn't expect to see you down here today." In fact, she had never been in his home, not since she'd been back, and he'd only lived here for a couple of years so it wasn't like there had been any other opportunity either. "I was going to come up to the house to talk to you."

She opened the cabinets, making herself right at home while she searched for a mug. Just as he was about to tell her the cupboard to the right, she discovered them and poured a mug. She held up the pot.

"Refill?"

Damn, she was cool. Her eyes were steady as if she'd sipped coffee with him a thousand mornings before today. He had to admit he wished he was as calm as she looked. And then he saw it; she was flicking her pinky under her thumb, something she only did when she was really nervous. He wanted to pull her into his arms and tell her nothing would hurt her as long as he was around, but he stayed where he was.

"No, thanks. I'm all set."

She glanced at the mug on the counter and filled it anyway. She flashed a smile at him. "It's almost empty."

The jig was up; she knew he was off-kilter now. Slowly he moved across the room and picked up the carton of cream and added some to his coffee and did the same to hers. "Sugar?"

"I'm good. Thanks." She gestured to the kitchen table. "Mind if we sit and talk a while?"

He pulled out a chair for her and sat on the other side. The room seemed to shrink with her in it. He could smell the vanilla scent of her shampoo as she tucked a short lock behind her ear. His heart skipped a beat as he noticed the pearl earrings she wore. Could they be the ones he gave her for her twenty-first birthday?

Silence between them grew as they both concentrated on their coffee. It was up to him to break the ice. "How was your trip?"

Her eyes met his over the rim of her mug and she set her cup aside. "Busy, but I got accomplished what needed to be done and I brought Daphne back with me. She's been wanting to come out to the ranch and now seemed like as good a time as any."

Yeah, before you sell the place? He pushed that thought aside. Linc had been looking for an opportunity where he could say his piece and Annie hadn't realized when she walked through the door that he wanted—no, he needed—to talk to her before she could break the bad news.

"Um, I'm happy to see you this morning. I was planning on going up to the house. You're right; we need to talk."

Her brows arched and her eyes widened for a half second before returning to normal. "I guess great minds do think alike. Would you mind if I go first?"

He knew a gentleman would agree, but he had to tell her before he lost his nerve. "What I need to tell you has waited too long. Give me five minutes?"

His heart slowed and his mouth went dry. She leaned back in her chair. "Of course, Lincoln. What's on your mind?"

He tented his fingers before placing his palms on the smooth wooden tabletop. His gut churned. It wasn't easy to guess how she'd react, but he knew because of his well-intentioned actions, he had changed the potential course of both their lives.

"I lied to you fifteen years ago." There. It was out in the open. He took a deep ragged breath and continued. "The last thing I wanted to do was break up with you before you went back East, but the way you talked about Boston and the life you were living, I knew I could never leave Montana. I was—no, I am—a rancher who loves wide-open spaces, harsh winters, hard work, and riding my horse across the plains. But it wasn't fair to expect you to give up what you obviously loved to come back to the ranch for me." He pushed his chair back and took her hand. "Come with me."

He could feel the warmth in her touch and

confusion filled her eyes. He wasn't sure if she wasn't speaking to let him finish or if she was in stunned silence.

He walked with her out the front door and stood next to the porch railing, looking out over the land.

"This is the only home I ever wanted and as much as I wanted you to be by my side, I couldn't let you sacrifice your future. I wanted you to live the life you were meant to have."

She pulled her trembling hand away and stuck it into the front pocket of her jeans.

He turned away from the view and watched her looking over her ranch.

"I never stopped loving you, Annie. There's never been another woman for me."

She took a side step away from him. He could feel the cool air separate them, but it was more like a raging river during the spring thaw. Her eyes were an icy blue and he was prepared for whatever she had to say; he deserved it.

"Do you have any idea what you've done, to me, to my life?" Her voice had a razor-sharp sting. "I've lived in Boston, away from the only family I had all those years, because you made a decision about my life and my future!" Her voice ratcheted up. "I was heartbroken when you said you wanted to date other girls. I was so embarrassed thinking I had misread all the signals from you. I stayed away from Grace Star Ranch and Pops because I never wanted him to be ashamed of me, pining for one of his ranch hands. And yes, I pined for you in the worst way. I just couldn't get over you."

That statement cut him to the quick, but he deserved her harsh words and more. He wanted to ask her if she had gotten him out of her heart.

"Every relationship I had was colored by what had happened." She paced the length of the porch, her boots thumping on the wooden planks. Each strike of the heel was a strike against his heart. She stopped and looked at him. "And now you're telling me that you've loved me for all these years and do you still?"

He dropped his chin and looked into her eyes. "Yes." One word was all he had to convey what was in his heart.

She shoved him out of her way and ran down the porch steps.

He started after her. "Annie, wait. We need to talk."

She whirled around, dust from the dirt path billowing up around her. "I came down here to tell you that I'm in love with you, hoping that you'd want to give us another chance. I've felt the chemistry between us; I'm not blind." She pointed at his chest. "And you have the audacity to state that you've always loved me, but you pushed me away so I could have a different life. Did you ever consider this might have been the life I would have chosen? Boston is a terrific city, and I loved going to college there, but you made decisions for me like I wasn't capable of making the right choice for my future."

"You've got it all wrong. I was afraid you'd walk away from an amazing opportunity to have a career to come back to the ranch to be with me."

"You're a jerk!" She turned to leave, and over her shoulder, she said, "And don't follow me. This time I'm making the decisions for my life, my future."

She stalked in the direction of the horse barn and Linc knew she was seeking solace with Bowie.

It was what she had always done; her horse was everything to her. He stood until the barn door slammed behind her, then he dropped to the porch steps. What was he going to do now?

A shrill whistle caught his attention and he turned in the direction of the sound. Mary was standing at the edge of the garden and gestured for him to follow her. Now he was going to get a tongue-lashing by the only woman who was tough enough to take him to task—well, besides Annie that is. With one long look at the barn, he walked up the knoll and through the garden gate.

Mary watched his approach with a withering gaze. She shook her head. "I could hear my girl all the way up here. I take it your confession wasn't met with her throwing her arms wide open and giving you a kiss."

"You guessed it. She's madder than a bull at a rodeo."

Mary made a soft *tsk, tsk* sound. "What exactly did you say and I'm not trying to come across as an old busybody, but I'd like to see the two of you come to some sort of a truce and I can't help you if I'm in the dark."

He perched on the edge of a raised bed and ran his hand through his hair. "In a nutshell I told her I lied all those years ago and I did it so she could have the life she deserved. Which as it turns out was what I shouldn't have said. Annie accused me of taking away her ability to make her own decisions and said because of my actions, she didn't come home much; she was embarrassed by it all."

"What do you think? Is it possible you were wrong even if your intentions were good?"

"When I was in my early twenties, I thought it was my place to do all I could to protect Annie and that included breaking up with her."

"In doing so, you broke her heart and forced her to make a choice she might not have wanted to make." She cut off a head of lettuce and put it into her basket before picking green beans.

Linc helped her pluck the bright-green pods from the vines. "Are you saying I was wrong?"

Mary worked silently, as if contemplating what to say next, or maybe in her usual style, she was forcing Linc to look inward and come to his own conclusion.

"Sometimes when we love someone, we screw

up, thinking we're doing the wrong thing for the right reason."

Now he got where she was coming from. He hadn't wanted to break up with Annie, but he thought he was doing the right thing for her and it had come from a place of love.

"Why did you wait so long to be honest with her? There were many times over the last fifteen years you could have reached out. If nothing else, it might have released you both to move on. Instead, neither of you has ever been able to do so."

"Mary, she seemed happy when she came home, like we were buddies, nothing more." Had she been acting like he had? His shoulders sagged as it all came crashing in. Not only had he been stupid for breaking it off, but he'd been an even bigger jerk in thinking she had been able to forget about him any more than he had forgotten her. He started remembering little things, like the way he'd catch her looking in his direction when she was riding with Pops, her eyes hidden by dark sunglasses and her Stetson. Or how he would look for a rental car around the holidays, hoping to catch a glimpse of Annie, and he always had a mixed bag of emotions when she was here alone. He had wanted her to be happy, but she never brought a man back to the ranch with her.

"I'll bet she's been as happy as you've been."

That simple statement was a like a horse shoe to his thick head—hard, painful, and shocking. He had been happy to a point, but half of his heart had lived over two thousand miles away and now it was only yards away. What was he doing? He straightened his spine. It didn't matter how mad she was at him; he needed to try one more time.

Mary's hand on his arm stopped him. "Listen not with your ears but with your heart."

He dropped a kiss on her cheek. "I will."

Chapter Seventeen

Annie ran a brush over Bowie's neck. She kept her voice soft as she poured her heart out to the mare. As was typical, Bowie just listened and leaned into her, offering comfort as well as companionship. If Annie hadn't known better, she'd swear the horse understood every word and agreed that Linc was a class A jerk.

"I can't believe he decided to make all the decisions for me. Who does he think he is? I wasn't his little woman that needed to be told what to do." She shook her head and moved to the opposite side, her back to the stable door. Beau came over and stood next to his momma and Annie ran the brush lightly over his back, pleased to see he didn't shy away from her. She needed to spend more time down here so the colt could become comfortable around her. After all, he was her hope for the future of her breeding program, especially if he grew up to have a good temperament and was easy to train as he already had the looks and bloodline.

"Time will tell, little boy." She gave him a pat and went back to brushing Bowie. After she finished, she walked into the office in search of a bag of carrots or apples and looked out the small window. Linc was headed in her direction.

She straightened her hat and strode out to cut him off. He stopped short when he was a few feet away from the door. He took his Stetson off and lowered his eyes before meeting hers.

"Annie, can we talk for a few minutes?"

What the heck? Hadn't he said enough already? "Sure. I have a few things I'd like to say to you." She heard the chill in her voice and although it wasn't normal for her to be so harsh, he deserved it. Single-handedly, he had changed the course of her life.

"Can we go for a walk?"

He usually asked to ride, not walk, but since living in Boston, she had discovered the therapeutic benefits of walking. She strode in the direction of the river. Maybe she could push him in if he really ticked her off. A small smile crept over her lips when she pictured him soaking wet as the water rushed around him. It would serve him right.

He fell in step beside her, and they walked in an uncomfortable silence for about a hundred yards before she looked his way. Her steps slowed. "What gave you the right to make decisions about my life without discussing them with me?"

"I was wrong." The sorrow she saw in his eyes cracked the shell of anger protecting her heart. "That's an understatement." She walked through the wooden gate, and he closed it behind them. The dry grass crunched under their boots as they walked down the two-lane gravel path through the field. "Did Pops know what you did?"

"He asked what happened between us, but I

told him to talk to you. You might think it was the coward's answer, but I wanted to give you an opportunity to tell him what you wanted."

"He asked and I said we had decided to each go our own way. Pops never asked again."

His hand brushed hers with a light touch. "If it makes a difference and I could go back, I'd do things different."

She didn't take his hand but didn't pull it away either; the warmth of his skin close to her was soothing. She longed to interlace their fingers, knowing they fit together like a hand and glove, but now was not the time to give in to what she desired.

With a heavy heart, she said, "We can't change the past, Linc." It was still a painful memory when he said it was time they both move on, but the final crushing blow to her heart was when he said what they had was puppy love, not real. Her feelings for him were deeper and more profound than any relationship since.

The sounds of the river washed over the jagged hurts of the past. This had always been their special place, sitting on the gravel bank with scrub grass at their backs. The bends of the riverbed had changed just as her life, but in some ways, it was still as familiar as always.

"We can change our future and I meant it when I said my feelings for you never changed. It wasn't love between kids but the real thing, at least for me." He stopped and took her hand. "Is it too late, Annie? Do you still care for me at all?"

How should she answer that? Be honest and tell him she loved him or skirt around the truth? She didn't answer him right away. Thoughts tumbled in her head. Could she trust him now with her heart? There were too many questions that needed answers.

"This morning I came down to talk about the future, for us and the ranch." She watched as a mask dropped over his face. She was confused; he'd said he still loved her but now his face was expressionless. What was his problem? She noticed the small wooden bench where they used to sit. He ambled in that direction and she followed.

"Is this bench new?" She hadn't been out here in years and suspected it was his handiwork and that meant this spot was still special to him. Or did she read it all wrong?

"It is. The old one rotted away."

She walked around him and took a seat. He sat close to her on the bench, their thighs almost touching.

"I'm curious what you wanted to say earlier, before I derailed the conversation."

Without hesitation, she began. "While I was gone, I thought a great deal about this ranch and the people who worked for me and you."

He looked out over the water. A fish jumped, but he remained motionless.

She took a deep breath. "It seems we're on the same trail. My feelings for you have grown stronger since I've been back and before life changes here on the ranch, I wanted you to know how I felt."

A muscle twitched in his clenched jaw.

"Look at me, Linc." She touched his chin and he turned. His hazel eyes were more muddy brown than gold today. "I'm afraid of getting hurt and that if I open my heart to you again, we'll have a repeat performance of you doing something you think is for my own good."

"And the ranch?"

"One thing at a time, cowboy. We need to talk about us." She wanted to see him grovel just a little bit. He was a proud man, but if he showed his tender side, it would help her trust him again. She waited.

He swung around on the bench and took her hands. "Because of me, we've lost years we'll never get back. I'm so sorry for what I did and I can't forgive myself, so how can you possibly forgive me?"

"This is a start." She gave him a small smile. "You're a good man and just saying you're sorry is the first step for both of us to forgive past hurts. And there's one thing Pops always told me. When you love someone, if they apologize for hurting you, forgiveness is an extension of that love." She traced his jawline with her fingers and his face relaxed under her touch. "I wasn't blameless. I put pressure on you to come with me and I never took into account that you wanted to be here." Her gaze swept the landscape. "It's your home."

"I am happy here, but there was a huge part of me that wanted to fly to Boston and be with you."

"But you stayed." Her voice was soft and she understood the push and pull of the heart. Especially in light of his admission of love.

"Do you think we can pick up where we left off?" He held her hand a little tighter and she heard the hope in his voice.

"No, we can't."

He dropped his head and nodded. "I understand."

"We're not the same people we were, but I'd say yes if you asked me out to dinner on a real date and see what remains between us."

He looked deep into her eyes and she could see the question lingering there. Leaning forward, she brushed her lips over his. He gave her the lead; like a skittish horse, he sensed she needed to take it slow.

"Would you like to have dinner with me tonight? We could go to the River Junction Inn; the Eastons own it now and they serve dinner. I've heard the food's good. I could pick you up at about five."

"Make it five thirty and you've got yourself a date." Her heart soared. They might have a chance to start over, but this time she wasn't a college girl with stars in her eyes. She was a woman who knew what and who she wanted in her life.

He slipped his arm around her shoulders and scooted closer to her. She didn't want to break the moment by saying she needed to get back to work. So with all thoughts pushed aside, she savored being in his arms. This was more important than paperwork.

Annie swished the skirt of her wine-colored A-line dress as she peered in the mirror and watched it move softly around her legs. She added a pin to the deep V-neckline since she didn't want to show off the girls to the world and then stepped into highly polished black Presidio cowboy boots decorated with tiny cutout dots that were really stars all over the boots. She sighed and thought of Pops indulging her love of hand-crafted boots; her closet was brimming with boots in varying heights, types of leather, and for all occasions.

These happen to be perfect for tonight, dressy but comfortable, and in some small way she felt closer to Pops tonight, and she needed that. Annie wished he were here to give her an encouraging hug. Linc had always been the name he dropped when she talked about dating someone new. Hugging her arms around her waist, she tried to remember what it felt like to get a bear hug from a giant of a man.

With a soft tap on the door, Daphne eased it open. With a side smile, she released a low wolf whistle. "You look amazing and I love those boots."

She stepped from side to side, showing off the boots right down to the soles. "They are pretty, aren't they?"

"And those stars are fitting, but I'm surprised you're not wearing heels."

"That's Boston Annie, and this Montana girl is happy to be wearing something that is borderline bedroom slippers as she steps out with a handsome guy for the night." She never really thought how there were different sides to her but now that she acknowledged it, slipping into jeans, cozy flannel shirts, boots, and her head covered by a cowboy hat was when she felt most comfortable in her skin.

"You need to go shopping and get some boots, along with some ranch wear for yourself. You'll never want to put on a dark suit and button-down blouse again." She placed a hand on Daphne's arm. "Trust me." She tapped her finger on her chin. "In fact, we'll go to the hardware store tomorrow and see what we can find."

"Is that the place you've been talking about?"

She laughed, and it felt good to let it rumble up from her belly. "Among other things. It'll be a blast."

"Where are you going tonight? Are there even great restaurants out here?"

"Now you're sounding like a snob. We have great places to dine. In fact, we're going to the River Run Inn; their restaurant is the Mountainside. And before you ask, it overlooks the mountain range and the views are stunning."

"Maybe we'll have time to go there before I have to leave."

Annie gave her best friend a hard hug. "We'll

have time to get all things in. But after we get you some new clothes, we'll go riding, poke around the ranch a bit, and enjoy all that Grace Star Ranch has to offer."

Daphne cocked her head and gave her a side-eye. "Annie, what are you plotting?"

She tapped her empty wrist where she had worn a watch back East. "Look at the time. Linc will be waiting on me. Don't wait up."

She grabbed a soft wool wrap and bag off the chair and felt as if she were floating down the hall. It was almost like a time warp, getting ready to see Linc. When she entered the living room, he was standing next to the mantle, looking at a picture of her and Pops taken a couple of years ago.

She didn't say anything but waited until he turned. The smile started at one side of his mouth and seemed to fill every part of his face and brighten his eyes. Then he held out his hand and stepped to her. Like a moth to a flame, she stepped into his arms and kissed him lightly on the cheek.

"You look amazing," he murmured in her ear. "Ready?" As he draped her wrap around her shoulders, his warm breath caressed her cheek. Would he kiss her again? She waited, hoping he would; however, he didn't. But she was pleased to see he wasn't just picking up where they once were, even if the heat that rushed over her was unmistakable and something she hadn't felt in a very long time.

His hand slid down her arm and he laced his fingers with hers. After fifteen years, it still felt like it was just yesterday.

"We have a reservation and I asked Becky if she'd put some of that white wine you like on ice."

She blinked. "You're willingly drinking white wine?"

His smile widened if that was possible. "I've got a few surprises in store for tonight and don't even think about asking what they might be." He pulled open the front door and they walked down the wide steps. "I want tonight to be memorable."

She looked around. "Where's your truck?"

"At my cabin. I thought you might want to ride in something a bit less practical." He pointed with their joined hands at the car parked in front of the house.

"You finished the Corvette?"

"And you're the very first woman to ever sit in it next to me."

He certainly was full of surprises. The Corvette was something that had just been a rust bucket when they found it in a field over twenty years ago. "I had no idea."

"A man's got to have a few surprises for a beautiful lady."

She liked how that sounded. Over the years, she had gotten some crow's feet and laugh lines and wondered if she still tripped his trigger, but by the look in his eyes, she'd have to say it was most definitely a yes.

Chapter Eighteen

Linc held the door to the inn while Annie walked in ahead of him. Becky met them at the podium with a welcoming smile and she clasped Annie's hands in hers. "You must be Annie Grace. Linc talks about you all the time."

He felt the heat creep up his neck. "Becky's stretching the truth just a little. You'll find out as you get to know her that she's the kind of person where the glass is overflowing all the time."

She gave him an easy smile. "There's nothing wrong with being an eternal optimist, Lincoln."

Annie chuckled at the exchange. "Becky put

you in your place," she said, then winked at the innkeeper. "I think we're going to be good friends."

"I hope so." She picked up menus. "Come this way and I'll show you to your table."

They arrived at a table next to a large picture window which looked out at the stunning mountain range. Annie glanced around the dining room; it was empty save for one other couple.

Linc held her chair as she took her seat and flashed him a sweet smile. Her eyes sparkled and he wondered if she knew the effect she had on him. He longed to sweep her in his arms and take her back to his cabin. *Slow down, cowboy. You still need to win her heart before you can plan something more.*

"I'll be right back with your wine." She placed a hand on Linc's shoulder before she whispered to him.

Annie's brow arched and her smile tipped in amusement. He was going all out tonight and he had mentioned there were other little surprises he had in store. She'd leave him to his secrets since he was confident she'd love each gesture.

She looked out the window. "The view is breathtaking. It's sad that it took Pops passing away for me to return home."

She let out a heavy sigh and he placed his hand over hers. That sigh. It was just like it had always been when she was carrying the weight of the world on her heart and her mind. Some things hadn't changed, and he was glad for the opportunity to support her.

Becky returned with the wine in a chiller bucket and placed it next to the table. She poured a small amount in each glass, then moved away after telling them to signal when they were ready to order.

They clinked their glasses, and he said, "To second chances." She smiled but a faraway look crept into her eyes.

"What are you thinking about?"

"How much time we've lost when we could have grown together."

He squeezed her hand. "I wish I could change the past, but all we have is this moment and the future as we decide what that might be."

She nodded and sipped her wine. "This

morning I wanted to talk to you about my plans for the ranch."

His gut clenched; was he ready for her to announce the changes?

"Do you remember when Lucas Gasperini came to the ranch a few weeks back?" She flicked her pale-pink napkin over her lap and rearranged her silverware next to her plate.

"Yes." He struggled to keep his voice neutral when he wanted to demand why she'd given up to sell out before seeing what the ranch could become under her leadership. But she needed to follow her heart and he wasn't going to try and change her mind, no matter what that meant.

She leaned forward and dropped her voice. "He gave me a great idea and I'm not sure if you noticed that I asked for his research to"—she did air quotes—"consider his proposal."

He gave a half nod and steeled himself for what was coming next. "I'm sure he dangled a lot of money in there too."

"Money is the driving factor for everyone." She propped her chin in the palm of her hand; her eyes held a glint of mischief. "I wanted to know what the viability was for a resort and why do the work when he was ready to hand it over to me for free."

He wasn't sure where she was going but her eyes shimmered with mischief.

"What do you think if we build a half dozen guest cabins and open a resort? It's why I brought Daphne out. She's at a crossroads in her life and I haven't asked her yet, but I want her to run that part of the ranch. Starting small will give us the opportunity to make it a very special experience and we could even have guests in the winter with snowmobiling, cross-country skiing, and maybe even trail rides. Based on Gasperini's research, we could be sitting on a gold mine. On top of all the winter activities, we have the best fishing spots. I could hire a guide who is passionate about hiking and outdoor sports."

Did this mean she'd be back more often? It sounded like the idea had potential and his heart held out a little hope. "Will it be hard to run the ranch and resort from Boston?"

Her mouth dropped open and she sat back in her chair. "What are you talking about?" She laughed. "Have you been under the impression that I'm leaving again and you were willing to start dating even though I might pack up?"

His insides began to untangle as her soft laughter was a salve for the wound on his heart. "Yes," came out more as a croak than a word. He cleared his throat.

"You're not the only one who has regrets. My greatest is that I wasn't able to run the ranch with Pops. Although I can't change my past choices, I want to bring his dream to fruition by living and working here and keeping his legacy alive. I'm the last member of the Grace family and I won't let Pops or my dad down. And if that means I open this place up as a part-time resort to bolster the ranch operation, then I will."

His heart pounded in his chest as he realized she was staying. "Do you need to go back to Boston and finalize everything?"

"What do you think I did for the last few weeks?" She gave him a wide grin. "I listed my place with a realtor, had the movers come and pack what I wanted to have here, and donated the rest. Oh, and as my final act of becoming a full-time rancher and resort owner, I handed in my resignation.”

“It’s official. You’re taking over the ranch and opening a resort!” He jumped out of his chair and pulled her into his arms, swinging her around.

She laughed and clasped her arms around his neck. “You might get sick of me hanging around, and by the way, I have a few more ideas.”

He set her down and kissed the palms of her hands. “I can’t wait to hear all of them, and I’ll do my best to make your dreams come true.”

She tipped her head and a tear clung to her eyelashes. “You’ve already started.” She withdrew her hand and picked up her wineglass. “I’d like to make another toast.”

He followed her lead and held up the glass with the sweet white wine.

“To our future, to whatever lies ahead, and to leaving our past behind and embracing what comes next in our future.”

They sipped the wine, and then he took her glass and pulled her close to his chest. With a tender touch, he brushed her hair back from her face. “I’m a simple man, but the only thing I’ve ever longed to have in my life is you. Tonight, you've made me very happy." He brushed his lips over hers.

Her small laugh made his soul soar. "If I had known it was this easy to make you smile, I'd have told you the news when you picked me up."

"Timing is everything, love." He should have held back the term of endearment, but it bubbled up from his toes. Forgetting they weren't alone in the room, he kissed her with everything that had been bottled up for the last fifteen years. Tender at first with the heat building, lost in the moment with her.

After several long seconds, she put a hand over his heart. "Let's enjoy our dinner and maybe we can pick this up later?" She wiped his mouth with her finger. "Deep pink isn't your shade."

Now that he had her in his arms, the last thing he wanted was to let her go, but she was right. There was plenty of time to kiss her lipstick off. He cupped her cheek and gazed into her eyes. "It looks great on you though."

He held out her chair and she picked her napkin up from the floor and set it aside.

Becky came over, and Linc said, "We'd like to take our time so there's no rush for anything."

She topped off their wine and took their order. From that moment onward, Annie and Linc shared stories about their lives, hopes, and dreams. Some of it reminded him of first date fodder but it was on a deeper level. He felt as if they were not just reconnecting but going much deeper. He never had any doubt that she was the stars in his night sky, but as dinner progressed, he knew he was not going to let her get away. If at some point she decided Montana wasn't for her, he'd pack his bags and follow her to the ends of the earth.

At the end of the evening, Linc took the long way back to the ranch, showing Annie all the new places that had sprung up on the outskirts of town, and he drove by River Bend Orchard.

"How's the apple orchard been doing?"

He slowed the car and pulled onto the shoulder of the road. "Right after you moved, the Mitchells expanded the orchard and planted more trees. Then about a year ago, their daughter Renee came back to run the place and she reconnected with Hank Sheppard—remember his family has a ranch west of town. He was a big shot lawyer in Dallas but moved back and now he's become a farmer."

She placed a hand over her heart as her face softened. "True love won out."

"Maybe we could take an afternoon this fall and pick apples?"

"I've never done that before but it's a date." She laughed. "And Mary can bake the pie."

He smacked his lips. "Or two." He pulled back on the two-lane road and turned for home. "Have you enjoyed tonight?"

"It's been amazing." She leaned over and kissed his cheek. "Tomorrow you should come up for breakfast and I can show you my ideas for the resort additions. But not a word to Daphne yet about her role. I plan on taking her for a ride and asking her if she'd consider joining my team."

He brought her hand to his lips and placed a kiss on the underside of her wrist. "Sounds good but I'm hoping for a little more time together before we call it a night." He looked into her eyes.

She kept her gaze steady. "I don't want to rush

whatever is developing between us. Can you give me some time?"

"Annie, you can have all the time in the world." He drove through the ranch gates. Even though he was disappointed, he was not about to screw this up.

The next morning Linc walked toward the main house when a cloud of dust following a luxury sedan stopped him in his tracks. A sinking feeling landed in the pit of his stomach. The last time a car like that showed up unannounced, it was the developer looking to sweet-talk Annie out of the ranch. He picked up the pace and reached the back door before the car parked out front.

Annie was at the breakfast table and her smile reached her eyes, welcoming him.

He kissed her. "You've got company out front."

She pushed back her chair. "I'm not expecting anyone." She crossed to the front room and looked at the high-end car.

"Are you thinking what I am? Lucas

Gasperini. He must be tired of waiting for my answer."

"What a way to start your day." He stood close to her and could feel the warmth of her body. "Do you want me to take off and come back later?"

She placed a hand on his arm. "Stay. The last time you hightailed it, you got the wrong impression. Besides, I'd like for you to see his face when I turn him down." Her wicked little grin reminded him how much she liked to throw down the gauntlet when she was squaring off against a strong adversary.

"I might feel sorry for this guy if he wasn't after the property. He has no idea what he's walking into."

She jabbed him in the ribs. "But on the other hand, he's lucky I've had two cups of coffee." She crossed to the front door and opened it as the car stopped under the portico. She didn't walk down the steps but waited for Gasperini to get out. Linc stood next to her but slightly behind, clearly indicating Annie was in charge.

"Annie, so nice to see you again." The older

gentleman hurried around the front of the car and up the wide steps. He was impeccably dressed in a leather jacket and designer jeans, right down to his pristine cowboy boots. Who was he trying to impress?

"Good morning, Lucas. I wasn't aware we had a meeting scheduled today."

Color flushed his face. "We didn't, but I was anxious to discuss my company acquiring the ranch." He jiggled the briefcase he held up, as if it would rattle with money. "And I have a new offer for you. I got the investors to sweeten the pot."

She stepped to one side and gave Linc a quick wink out of Gasperini's view. "You remember my ranch manager, Lincoln Cooper. Won't you please join us for coffee."

Lucas shook his outstretched hand. "Pleasure to see you again."

Annie pushed open the door and he let Gasperini go in ahead of him. He looked to his right and left. It was easy to see he noticed the stonework on the fireplace and large windows with sweeping views of the ranch, almost as if he were assessing the place.

"We won't have to change much in the main house."

And there it was. Annie didn't respond to the comment, but instead, said, "Let's sit in the living room where we'll be more comfortable." She gestured for Linc and Gasperini to take a seat before leaving the room.

He leaned closer to Linc. "I'll bet she's excited for the next phase in her life. I'm about to make her a very wealthy woman. It'll be much easier negotiating with her than her grandfather."

Linc propped his boot-covered ankle on the opposite knee. This really was going to be fun to watch. Annie was more like Pops than she realized, and this pushy man was about to find out just how much.

"Annie is very excited to talk with you and begin her future." He lifted his eyes as she walked in carrying a tray. Before he could get up and take it from her, it was already on the table.

Annie looked at Linc before her intense gaze settled on Mr. Gasperini. "Shall we get down to business?"

Chapter Nineteen

Annie took her time and poured three mugs of coffee. Out of the corner of her eye she could see a tiny smirk on Linc's face. Heavens, but that man knew her well. She passed the mugs to both men and then took hers and eased back in the stiff-armed chair. No sense getting too comfortable. Mr. Lucas Gasperini wasn't going to be staying long.

"Lucas, I'm surprised you drove all the way out here so early this morning. Did you drive in from Bozeman?"

"No, I stayed at a charming establishment. River Run Inn. Do you know it?"

He slurped his coffee which grated on a nerve; it was one of her pet peeves.

"Yes, it is charming." She wasn't about to mention they had dinner there last night. There was no point in idle chitchat.

He looked out the window. "It is beautiful here and it will make a wonderful vacation destination."

"You're talking as if I've signed on the dotted line and cashed your check." There was a deliberate chill in her tone and one she didn't try to warm up. This jerk was really ticking her off and it was way too early in the day to be mad, especially since she was looking forward to a nice breakfast with her handsome guy. She looked at Linc who was casually sipping coffee, his arm draped over the back of the sofa. To an onlooker, he might look disengaged, but she knew he didn't miss a trick or a syllable.

"I'm confident once you see the offer, you'll be eager to sign." He withdrew a thick contract and flipped through it before handing it to her along with a Mont Blanc pen. "The terms are at the top of the page."

She took the contract. "I'll need to get my reading glasses." She casually tossed the contract on the gleaming pine table and left the room. This was more for dramatic effect than needing her glasses, but she'd let him sweat for a minute, and then it would be over and breakfast would be back in play.

Her office was at the end of the hallway, and after picking up her glasses, she looked at the framed picture of Pops on the corner of her desk. "Don't worry. I'm your granddaughter and after the next five minutes are history, this guy won't make a return visit to Grace Star." She kissed her fingertips and touched the glass.

Upon entering the living room again, there was no idle conversation, just an awkward silence. She picked up the contract and slid her glasses into place on her nose but didn't sit down. Instead, she walked to the front window. She scanned the page and was shocked at the amount of money offered but that didn't give her second thoughts as it only reinforced that under her control, she could grow the ranch on many levels and in the process keep her current people on the payroll, help Daphne, and help the town. There were other ideas niggling at the back of her mind to help other businesses grow from the increased visitor traffic. But it would all take time and planning; the first she had years to accomplish, and the second she'd bring in whomever she needed to make it happen.

Lucas cleared his throat. "Um, Annie, do you have any questions before you sign?"

She suppressed the smile on her lips before she slowly turned, hoping to make him squirm just a tad. There was no reason to pretend that she was pleased he had been so audacious and just showed up uninvited.

She kept her face neutral and her voice steady. "Lucas, the terms are extremely generous, but I'm afraid I can't sign." She tore the contract in half and handed him the pieces. "I have no intention of selling Grace Star Ranch to you or anyone else for that matter. This is my home, not a simple business transaction."

"But I thought you were from Boston. Surely you realize you can't run an operation this size remotely."

It wasn't a question but a snarky statement and one he had sorely misjudged.

"Allow me to refresh your memory; you struck out with John Grace, my grandfather, and now you've struck out with me. I would suggest you go back to your group of investors and tell them there is no deal for my land." She didn't dare look at Linc because she was sure he was beaming since he didn't care for Mr. Gasperini's tactics.

"I think you'll regret not selling to me, just as River Bend Orchard will come to regret it too. I'll just buy another ranch and it will be successful."

"That's your prerogative. It's time for you to leave, and if I can give you a friendly piece of advice; the next time you think to drop by and dangle money in front of a landowner, you might want to set up a meeting first. Dropping by is rude, especially since we have a ranch to run."

She crossed to the front door and opened it. "Good day, Mr. Gasperini."

He set his coffee mug down with a thump and snatched up his briefcase. He paused in front of Annie, clutching the ripped-up contract. "My offer will stand for twenty-four hours. Call me if you have a change of heart."

She nodded to his car. "My answer is set in concrete. Safe travels."

Linc came up behind her as she walked onto the porch and watched the retreating car and the gravel that was kicked up as Gasperini drove off.

She slipped her arm around his waist and laughed softly. "So, what do you think? Would Pops have approved of how I handled our guest?"

He placed a kiss on the top of her head. "Are you kidding? You are one tough businesswoman and I'm excited to see where you're going to take this ranch. I predict great things are on the horizon."

"What was that about the orchard?"

"Rumor has it last year he went poking around, heard Renee was struggling a bit, and swooped in and tried to buy the orchard. She stood her ground and basically did the same as you. From what Hank said, all he needed to do was mention he was Renee's lawyer and the guy took off."

"Maybe we should let other ranches and businesspeople know this guy is nosing around. I'd sure hate for anyone to get taken advantage of."

"I'll give Hank a call and between us we can get the word out, but at some point, someone's gonna sell to him."

"Then we'll make sure at least whoever it is will be informed first." She waited until the car disappeared around the last bend before she said, "I'm starving. Let's go see if Mary is up for making waffles today; I think they'd hit the spot." She patted her midsection and gave him a side-look.

"That sounds good," Linc said.

"And then we both have work to do. I need to convince Daphne to leave Boston, hire an architect, and map out plans for the cabins. If you're interested, come for dinner and I'll reveal my grand scheme to conquer the world."

"You can count on me." He stopped walking and gave her a serious look. "Mary's definitely cooking?"

With a playful shove, she said, "Of course. I'm not about to try and score points with my cooking; she's the best." She placed a finger across her lips. "But don't tell Quinn I said that; he's a close second."

He claimed her lips and said, "I'll keep all your secrets safe."

After a morning filled with answering emails, Annie checked on the garden. She was thrilled to see Polly's progress. Polly was leaning against the fence as Annie walked up. When she saw Annie, she walked over. "How's our garden growing?"

"Hey, Annie. Considering we got a late start, it's going great. I talked to Quinn about what we can preserve, and I did some updating to the old root cellar for storing the potatoes and onions. Next season will be better since I'll work the soil after the harvest in preparation of spring planting."

She nodded. "Excellent. And what about a greenhouse? I'd like to bring you on in a full-time capacity. Your primary responsibility would be the vegetable gardens, but in addition, I have some bigger plans that I think you could work into if you're interested."

Her eyes widened and a deep pink flushed her cheeks. "That would be awesome, and I've been thinking about a greenhouse and what size we'd need. I've sketched some ideas, you know the scope and location. I can bring them out tomorrow and show you."

Annie appreciated her enthusiasm and said so. Before Polly went back to work, she asked, "Will it be a requirement that I live on the ranch? Last fall I bought a small house I've been fixing up, and well, it's the first place that's really mine."

Surprised at the question, Annie smiled. "You can live wherever you want. We provide housing to the ranch hands as part of their salary. But if one of the hands wanted to live off the ranch, they could."

"Awesome. Thanks again, Annie, for the job and everything. Now I need to get back to work." She picked up a garden cultivator and began to turn the earth over.

Awesome must be Polly's favorite word. She'd used it a couple of times in this conversation alone. Annie glanced over her shoulder and from the smile on the woman's face, it was easy to see she was in her element. Everyone needed to find where they belonged in life. After a detour to see Bowie and Beau, she was going to saddle up two horses for her and Daphne. It was time to put her next part of the plan into action.

Annie and Daphne were on two of the tamer mounts from the stable. That was something Annie had to add to her ever-growing to-do list—horses for trail rides and maybe even a few ponies, in case any families made their way to Grace Star Ranch.

"I had forgotten how beautiful it is at the ranch."

Annie could hear the relaxed tone in Daphne's voice. The horses plodded along at a slow pace. She wasn't in a rush for them to get anywhere, and since Daphne hadn't been on a horse in at least five years, it was better to take it easy.

"I didn't realize how much I had missed this place until I made the decision to move home." She drank in the sights and sounds of the land. In the distance, the white-capped mountain range reminded her that everything in life had a season. It was summer now but soon enough the leaves would be changing, and she would need to have broken ground by then if she had any chance of welcoming guests next summer.

Annie pushed her straw cowboy hat off and glanced at Daphne. "There's something I've been wanting to talk to you about since you told me about your job."

Daphne's shoulders sagged. "It's been rough, but I'd rather just enjoy my vacation and think about that next week."

"What would you say if I asked you to stay here, at the ranch with me, and quit that crappy job?" A breeze kicked up and teased a strand of hair across her face. She tucked it behind her ear and made sure her hat was secure.

"It would be fun to stay out here, but I have bills to pay, and I'm going to guess there isn't a huge need for an event coordinator." She flashed her a grateful smile. "But thanks for the offer."

Annie tapped her heels against her mount,

and he eased into a gentle trot. "That's not the offer."

Daphne's horse picked up her pace, keeping abreast with Annie's. They headed across an open field. Annie had an area where they could look back over the main house, barns, and outbuildings. She wanted to paint a picture for Daphne so it would be impossible for her to say no.

As they came upon a couple of folding chairs and a small table set with a thermos and a container of cookies, Daphne laughed. "How did you get this set up? I've been with you since before lunch."

"Linc took care of it for me." She pulled the horse to a stop next to the fence, hopped down, and flicked the reins around the rail. She held the pinto while Daphne dismounted and secured him too.

"This is so nice, just like a tea party when I was a kid." She stretched her legs out in front of her while Annie poured their coffee. "I could get used to this."

That was a promising statement. She opened

the cookie container and held it out. Daphne took one and groaned softly as she bit into it.

"These are amazing. Snickerdoodles are my favorites."

After a few minutes of letting the scenery work its magic and the crisp, clean air waft around them, Daphne said, "I'm so glad you convinced me to come out with you. It's so peaceful here."

"That's because we're the only people around for a couple of miles." She glanced at her friend. "I have a proposition for you."

"If it's more adventures like this, count me in." She wiped the crumbs from the corner of her mouth and smiled. "Any chance Mary would make some cookies I could take with me when I leave?"

"I'm sure she'll make you all the cookies you want, but if you accept my proposal, you can have cookies and her meals." A grin filled her face.

"What are you talking about?" Daphne sat up straight in her chair.

"Do you remember I told you about the guy who wanted to buy the ranch and open a resort?"

"Sure, but you're never going to take the offer."

"Nope. I'm going to build some cabins and open my own working dude ranch slash resort and I want you to run all the events. Before that happens, I need to build it so they'll come, and I want you to be here from the beginning."

Her mouth dropped open. "You want me to move to Montana and work for you?"

Annie wasn't sure if she was excited, surprised, or upset. The tone of her voice was flat, devoid of emotion.

"That was the idea. But if making this kind of a change just isn't something that you'd want to consider, it's fine." Her excitement waned a bit; she thought Daphne would jump at the chance but instead, the suggestion was met with lukewarm enthusiasm at best. Annie took another cookie and nibbled on the crispy edge.

"Are you serious?"

Glancing her way, Annie grinned. "Of course I am. When it comes to my ranch, I want the best people in place and if it goes well, we might expand into heaven only knows what. Cattle ranching is one revenue stream, but I need to have other sources of income if there's a bad year for feed prices, shortages, or low beef prices. I need to keep everyone whole."

Daphne clasped her hands together in her lap. "It's a big responsibility. What if I'm not up to the job?"

"Does that mean you'll consider it?" Annie waited with bated breath. Her plans didn't hinge on if Daphne said yes, but this was a fresh start for both of them and there was no one she'd rather have working by her side.

Daphne shrugged her shoulders and threw up her hands. "What the heck, I'm all in."

Annie jumped up. "You're staying?"

Daphne stuck out her hand. "I accept your offer with one condition. If either of us ever thinks we need to stop working together and just be friends, there will be no hard feelings."

Instead of shaking hands, she threw her arms around Daphne and hugged her tight. "This is going to be the best thing for both of us."

Chapter Twenty

With a spring in his step, Linc made his way to the main house a week after Annie informed Gasperini she wasn't selling the ranch. He wanted to start his day by asking Annie on a date and do something special. That meant it was time to have a night under the stars. They had dinner together the last few nights, and Mary and Daphne had joined them. Not that he didn't like their company, but he had been wanting a little alone time with his girl.

He smiled when he thought of Annie as the woman who found her way into his heart so many years ago and she was like a loveable burr that stuck on a saddle blanket, almost impossible to get rid of without ripping the fabric. He laughed out loud; how would she like being compared to a prickly weed?

Mary popped up from behind the garden fence. "What's made you chuckle?"

He hadn't expected anyone to hear him, but since she had, Linc wasn't about to reveal the truth. "Hi, Mary. What are you doing out here so early?"

"I was cutting some chives for omelets. Are you hungry?"

He opened a side gate and crossed the space to take her woven basket. "When am I not? But I had breakfast in the dining hall. Quinn made flapjacks and sausage and I ate my share, but I'd love a mug of coffee."

She led the way to the kitchen and over her shoulder, she said, "Annie's in her office if you want to wander down."

Without a look back, Linc strode down the hall and tapped on the half-closed door before pushing it open. Expecting to see her at the desk, he wasn't surprised to see her looking out over the land, so much like Pops in many ways but also different in others. He'd be proud to see his granddaughter taking charge. "Good morning, Annie."

She smiled at him from over her shoulder. "Hey, handsome. Come over here and give me a proper hello."

Her come-hither smile was all he needed for encouragement. He slid his arms around her waist and lowered his lips to hers, kissing her until she laughed softly.

"Now that's what I call a hello."

He looked into her eyes. "I can make it a point to swing by bright and early every morning to help you greet the day."

His pulse quickened and he really wanted to say he'd love to wake up next to her and greet the day, but mentally he pulled back on the reins. He'd been pining for her for years, but he knew she'd had a few relationships. He was curious why one had never stuck; one day he'd ask her. Was it possible she hadn't ever gotten over him?

"Hey, why the frown?" She gave him a playful pat on his back.

He pushed the thought away. "It's nothing." He dropped a tender kiss on her cheek. "What have you been thinking about?"

She eased from his arms and opened the glass door to step outside. He followed her and took in the breathtaking vista.

"I was trying to think about how this view will change when I build the cabins and I'm not sure if that's what I want to look at from my office." She tapped her chin with her finger. "What if I carve out a section of pasture land down closer to the main road but still within sight of the barns and paddock? If I did, I'd have room to expand into more cabins if I found the need."

"Have you decided how many you want to build now?" He had no idea if she was starting small or going big; either way was in her scope based on the conversations they've had so far.

"Well, therein lies my first problem. Do I start by catering to couples with cabins for two, so they'd be a one-bedroom with a living space, a decent-size bath, and a small kitchenette? Even though I expect people will want the full ranch experience and dine at the hall with the hands milling around. Or do I add two cabins that could sleep up to six people, to include family groups, a couple with kids, or maybe a small group of friends? The cabins need to be comfortable but rustic at the same time; you know the best of both worlds."

He could see the excitement written all over her face. Her eyes sparkled; her cheeks were rosy, and she talked as fast as the words could tumble out. Her energy was just what the ranch needed. Things had been way too predictable for too long.

"Do you have a budget for the cabins and the enhancement for the dining hall and stables? And you're also talking about the greenhouse, another significant expense. Would it be best to figure out the finances first before making any decisions?"

"I did that when I was in Boston and since I had Gasperini's research, I knew his plan would need to be scaled back since I'm not razing any of the existing cabins or barns."

A dark cloud hovered over Linc's face. "What are you talking about? When he talked to Pops, there was no mention of demolishing any part of the ranch."

"I never saw the original proposal, but in this one the renderings of the property he included were missing some buildings. That's why I'm trying to decide the best place for the cabins."

She easily had dismissed the proposal and he should as well. In his gut he knew that was ancient history and she was like a charging bull with one exception; she had a plan.

"I'm glad you clued me in on what you're not doing, but think of the cabin location carefully. Do you want to drive past a bunch of cabins on your way home or would it be better to give your guests the full ranch view the minute they drive onto the property?" He held out his hand. "Come with me."

They walked down the hall and out onto the front porch. He stood behind her and pointed to the left first. "Close your eyes and imagine you're sitting on the swing, sipping a cool beverage, and a couple of cars pull in just near those stands of Ponderosa pines over yonder. People spill out of cars with bags and are chattering like magpies. Your peace and quiet evaporates. But now, the road to the cabin veers off farther down toward the road and they wind around the back side of the main house, but not where you can see them since you'll plant a living fence and then end at the cabins on the other side of the dining hall. They're stepping out into the action of horses meandering through with cowboys, and food is close by. We could put a small picnic area there and maybe down the road a playground for kids, cowboy-themed of course, and then it would be the best of both worlds and there'd be room to expand in that direction with even more cabins if you felt the need, all the while keeping your privacy intact."

She nodded. "I don't think I'd want to grow much beyond ten cabins."

"Then start with five, and maybe one is a larger unit. And also if for any reason you decide the resort isn't working, the new cabins are close enough you could use them for ranch hands who might want to continue to live at the ranch after they get married."

She leaned into his side and hugged him. "That all sounds good, but why did you mention about married ranch hands living here? I always thought they were anxious to move into town and buy a home."

"Times are a-changing and I've heard a couple of guys say they'd never want to live anywhere but the ranch, but one or two of them are thinking about settling down one of these days."

"Hmm, thanks for clueing me in. That does give me something else to consider." She scanned the property. "You have some great ideas. Care to be in the conversation with the architect when she comes out?"

"Nope. I'm happy to share any ideas I have with you and you're always able to bounce things off of me, but the expansion is your baby." He pecked her lips. "And I'll handle the ranch." He slung his arm around her shoulders and pulled her closer. "Okay?"

When she looked at him, his heart skittered in his chest. What he hadn't said was he was one of those guys thinking about long-range plans of set-tling down with the woman he loved.

"Got time for a cup of coffee or do you have pressing ranch business to attend to?" Her lips tipped up in a smirk and she dropped her voice. "I've heard the boss is one tough cookie."

"With a marshmallow center." He scooped her up and twirled her around until she laughed. "Mocking me now?" He set her down and kissed her one last time. If he accepted the coffee, even though Mary had offered him a mug as well, he'd never get to work, and there was much to do. There was haying equipment that needed to be repaired and the irrigation system in the west field was having some issues based on the logs he had reviewed earlier this morning, and a hay field needed to be checked for its first cutting. Just another day in the life of a rancher, but spending a few more minutes with Annie was worth pushing himself harder later.

She held up her thumb and forefinger with a small space in between them. "Maybe just a little."

"Come on, woman. Let's find that coffee and add just a little more spunk to you."

"You got it, dude." She gave him an exaggerated wink. "For the record, you're welcome."

With a hearty laugh, they went inside. She was going to keep him on his toes. "Oh, the real reason

I came up was to ask if you wanted to have dinner with me tonight. I thought we'd go down by the river and eat while the stars put on a show."

"I'd love to. I can make us a picnic." She closed the door behind them.

"I'll take care of everything. I'll pick you up at seven?" They stepped into the kitchen where Mary and Daphne were having breakfast.

After exchanging good mornings, Annie said, "We're going out tonight and Linc is picking me up for a picnic so I won't be home for dinner."

Daphne grinned. "A romantic dinner tonight under the stars. Very nice."

Mary beamed like it had been her idea. "I'll fry you up some chicken and all the fixings."

Linc dropped a kiss on her cheek. "No need, Mary. I've got it all taken care of, but thank you. Not that my food holds a candle to yours, but I'm sure you understand."

Mary actually blushed a little. "I do and if you change your mind, just let me know. I'm always happy to lend cupid a helping hand."

Annie held up her hand. "Excuse me, I'm standing right here, and Mary, you remember what the doctor said. With your blood pressure and cholesterol on the high side, you need to cut back on fried foods so we'll skip that for the foreseeable future."

"I know that, child, but Linc needs to have some mothering too. Besides, I wasn't saying we'd have it for dinner, but I'd make it for the love birds."

With a chuckle, he started to reply when his walkie squawked. "Boss, are you at the house?"

It was Clint. He pulled it from his belt. "Roger that."

"Meet me in your office in ten?"

"Copy that." He stuck the walkie in his shirt pocket and brushed Annie's lips with his. "I gotta run but see you at seven."

She clasped his hand and gave it a warm squeeze. "I'm looking forward to it."

He closed the door behind him and jogged to the dining hall, hoping nothing had gone wrong with the baler. He still needed to get to the river and set the scene including the fire pit. He had a few ways to keep his lady love warm, but the fire was for ambience and heat was secondary.

. . .

Linc tapped on the front door of Annie's home. He was dressed in a long-sleeve shirt, jeans, boots, and he had a denim jacket on the seat of the UTV. The door swung open and his breath caught. She was wearing jeans, old scuffed brown boots, a pale-blue chambray shirt open at the throat with the turquoise and bead necklace he had given her when she turned eighteen. A suede jacket was on the bench behind her and on her head a shallow-brimmed brown fedora. She remembered nights could be cool especially by the river.

"You look"—his mouth was dry and the words came out sounding more like a croak—"stunning."

She did a mock curtsy. "Thank you, and you're looking pretty sharp yourself. Two ranch folk dressed up for a night out on the town." She peeked around him. "And clear skies to boot."

He could have looked at her forever, but she grabbed her coat and pulled the door closed.

"Are we riding tonight?"

"No, I thought we'd drive out. This way no

matter what time we come home, we don't need to put the horses away for the night."

She tapped her temple. "You're a smart man." Before going down the steps, she stood on her tip-toes and her lips brushed his in greeting.

He liked the way she communicated without words and it matched how he felt as well. He poured his heart into the slow, simmering kiss. Her eyelashes fluttered as she looked into his eyes.

"Ready to go?" He took her hand and once settled into the UTV, he set off at a sedate pace. There was no sense of urgency for the night to be over.

"I'm glad we're picnicking tonight, but Mary would have whipped us up a nice dinner."

He gave her a sidelong look. "No need for you to worry about my cooking skills. Quinn saw me in the kitchen and jumped in to help so every-thing will be delicious."

She laughed heartily. "I thought you could cook."

"I can feed myself if necessary but why bother since Quinn has skills I'll never master."

"That's how I feel about Mary, but she's getting older and I want her to slow down, so I may need to get cooking tips from Quinn so I can keep us fed."

He turned on the path that led to the riverbank, and out of the corner of his eye he saw her smile. He was glad this was the spot that he'd chosen for tonight, but there were hundreds of perfect places to stargaze.

"It is so good to be home."

It wasn't something he needed to reply to. It came from her heart, a simple statement of all being right in their world.

Chapter Twenty-One

Annie wanted to pinch herself. Two weeks ago, she would never have pictured her and Linc zipping along over the path for a picnic and then doing one of her favorite things ever, watching the stars put on a show in the inky black sky. Montana wasn't called Big Sky Country for no reason and she was partial to the view from this ranch. While she was in Boston, other than Pops and Bowie, this is what she had missed the most—the openness, the solitude, and the wonder that appeared night after night over Grace Star Ranch.

She briefly thought of how they could capture

this for guests but silently admonished herself. Tonight wasn't about work; it was about the man sitting next to her, holding her hand and causing the butterflies in her belly to take flight. "In case I forget, thank you for tonight and for being honest with me about how you truly felt. When Mary encouraged me to go to you and tell you that I still cared for you, I thought you'd laugh in my face."

He glanced at her and gave her hand a gentle tug. "Then if you were concerned about the outcome, why did you come to see me?"

It was time to tell him she was ready to finally let the past go. But did she want to confess her greatest fear on such a beautiful night? It must be done to move forward. "If you knew and didn't want me to be a part of your life in that way, I could finally bury the past. I'd hoped you would reach out, and when you didn't, I never forgot about you."

"Pops always encouraged me to fly to Boston. He even offered to buy my ticket, as long as it was one way." He grinned at her. "I guess he thought once I got there I'd want to stay."

"You would have hated the city." She looked

around. "Tall buildings and it had a distinct odor. I mean, you get used to it, but still. On the plus side, the Atlantic Ocean is right there so going to the beach and eating fresh seafood was a treat. Oh, and concerts, movies, and events were so close, in most cases a T ride away."

He pulled his hand away and with it the warmth that had kept her heart swaddled in comfort. "Will you miss it?"

She thought about how best to answer his question, but then didn't censor herself. If they were going to have a chance to make it, she had to be totally honest. Despite her gut tightening and her anxiety ramping up, they both deserved her direct response.

"Part of me will miss Boston, the convenience to the stores, meeting friends on the spur of the moment, and I did love going out to dinner." She could sense Linc's withdrawal as she talked. "But this is my home and I'm not going anywhere again. I can take vacations and see the ocean, or heck, I can have seafood flown in if I get a hankering, but there isn't any way to replicate my hometown, the people I love and who love me, and living my best life right here."

He slowed the vehicle as he drew up to the riverbank and flipped the switch to off but didn't get out. "Are you sure ranch life will be enough for you?"

She took his hand and applied gentle pressure. "I went to college, never intending on leaving permanently. My goal was to get an education that I could apply to ranch life so Pops and I could grow this business together. But when you broke it off with me, I stayed back East to lick my wounds and it got easier to just stay away."

"I know I've said it before, but I wish I could go back to younger me and have the maturity I do now. I'd have never broken up with you just to give you the freedom I thought you needed."

"Fess up. You were scared and decided it was easier to say you wanted to date others instead of being honest." She watched as color crept up from his neck to his hairline. He needed to cowboy up and she'd wait.

Annie looked out at the river flowing over rocks, causing gentle ripples in the surface of the slow-moving water and he did the same. She wasn't getting out of the UTV until they put this to rest. She felt they had almost exhausted the topic, but there was one final point she wanted him to recognize. She wasn't trying to rub salt in the wound, but facing the mistakes of their past would hopefully mean they wouldn't be repeated down the road.

He cleared his throat. "I was scared. What if you went back and met someone who was a better man than me? I was scared of losing you. I'm not proud of being a coward and I should have let things play out. Instead, I ended our relationship on my terms. It was easier for me to be the jerk than be played a fool."

Now she was confused. "What kind of woman did you think I was? We were in a committed relationship and I would never have cheated on you. I loved you."

If he noticed she had used the past tense, he didn't react. But they were talking about then, not now. Today she loved him with fresh eyes, for the man he'd become and the woman she had matured into. He had been right. Even if it took time to admit it, they weren't ready to walk down an aisle back then, and he would have popped the question before she was ready; she knew it in her soul.

"I always thought I was a strong man, but you bring me to my knees, expose my soft side, and I didn't want anyone else to see me vulnerable."

"Do you think you're the first or last man to have a woman get under his skin?" Now she was making the presumption, but she knew it had hit the mark when his eyes met hers. There was no mistaking exactly how he felt about her still. He loved her. Her heart constricted. She didn't need to hear those words tonight, nor was she ready to say them. It was enough they felt them.

"No, but am I the only man to have gotten under yours?"

She felt the quick gut punch. Once again, she would be honest. "There was a guy who I was pretty serious about, but I didn't tell Pops, which should in itself speak of where my head was. That relationship was never like it was with us."

"Was he a good man?"

She slid across the bench seat, and he slipped his arm around her shoulders.

"He was, which is why I broke it off. He deserved someone who loved him with her whole heart, not just a sliver. It was then that I knew I'd left mine in Montana when I went to Boston. Which is why, if you turned me down and said you didn't have feelings for me, I would have let my heart finally heal."

He brushed her lips with his. "How's your heart today?"

"Recovering nicely, thank you very much." She deepened the kiss and her heart seemed to expand in her chest. They had given each other their hearts so long ago. Now it was time for them to let their love flow over the pebbles and boulders of life, much like the river that ran along in front of them. Time slowed and the world fell away. She was warm in his arms but more than that, she was loved.

The fire crackled and popped as they sat on a thick blanket on the grassy bank. The sun had set and the stars were beginning to make their appearance. Annie sat between Linc's legs and had tossed her hat to one side before she leaned her head against his broad chest. She sighed with deep contentment and inhaled the crisp, clean air.

"I can't believe it's almost July. Fall will be here soon."

"Usually does in these parts. But we'll be ready; we always are."

"Do we need to do anything special before the snow flies?" It had been almost twenty years since she'd witnessed the change of seasons out here, but she'd never forgotten what snowstorms could be like. She shivered, remembering if they weren't prepared it could cost livestock and even people their lives.

"Are you cold?" He tightened his arms around her.

"No, just realizing there is a lot riding on our being prepared. This will be the first winter without Pops guiding the team." She felt the sadness swamp her that she hadn't been able to help him take care of everything.

"He wasn't able to do much last year and he

relied on me and Clint to pitch in and do what he couldn't, and of course Mary kept track of everyone and reported back to Pops over dinner every night."

That was new information. She thought about all the years Mary and Pops had lived in the main house together. "Linc, do you think there was a closeness between them that I wasn't aware of?"

He was quiet for a long minute. "No, I don't think so, out of respect for your grandmother. But they were best of friends and she would have given her last breath if she thought it would have saved him."

"That's a special kind of love." She was in awe of Mary more and more every day.

"I know she's not your blood, but you're like her in many ways."

That was the nicest compliment she'd ever heard. Mary had been her role model for years, but she never thought she could measure up to her amazing qualities. "I'm not sure what to say other than thank you." She did wonder if the mere fact she never stopped loving Linc was similar to how Mary hadn't ever stopped loving her husband.

"Look."

She gazed over to where he was pointing. "The Big Dipper." She tipped her head back and smiled at him. "I remember the first time you tried to teach me about the constellations and all I wanted to do was spend the night kissing."

"And I had to keep diverting you since I would have needed a long cold shower or a dip in the river when I got home."

She laughed softly. Teen hormones raged until they had finally given in to what they both wanted, but he had always let her set the pace and he was happy to follow.

"We've come full circle, haven't we?" She thought even now he was the gentleman and letting her set the pace for their physical relationship. As much as she'd like to ask him to spend the night, a part of her wanted to hold back and let the anticipation of that moment build. She could wait—well, for now anyway.

"With wisdom comes a new beginning." The fire was beginning to burn down. "Do you want me to put another log on or are you ready to head out soon?"

"What time is it? I need to drive Daphne to the airport tomorrow, but she'll be back in a few weeks and then meet with an architect in Bozeman."

"That answered my question."

He wrapped his arms around her and kissed her neck, sending a tingle racing down her arms. She turned and pushed him back on the blanket with a playful shove. Without saying a word, she wanted to show him just what he meant to her by pouring her love into the kisses.

In the distance a coyote howled at the moon and she paused. "By any chance did you bring a pistol with us tonight?"

"Darlin', your safety is of the utmost importance. I have two firearms with me, just in case."

She eased back from his body. "Good and one thing I want to do is have you give me a refresher course at the firing range. It's been a while since I've handled a gun, and now that I'm home, I want to be able to shoot straight should I need to."

He didn't argue with her since he knew she often went out riding and she might just cross an ornery bear or wildcat. Not that she'd ever kill an animal unless it was to save herself or her horse, but just the crack of a bullet being fired was often enough to make a predator move along.

"I can do that." He helped her up, then she folded the blanket while he kicked dirt on what was left of the fire. Before she could pick up the basket, he pulled her to his chest and cupped her cheek in his hand. "Annie"—he searched her eyes in the moonlight—"I will spend the rest of my life making it up to you for the past. I've never stopped loving you and I never will."

"Sweetheart, after tonight, we're not talking about the past anymore. We were young and inexperienced and I love you for trying to do what you felt was right. For the rest of our lives, you have to promise that you'll talk to me and never make any decisions without discussing them with me. There isn't anything we can't talk about."

"I know that now. I just wish…"

The words died on his lips as she placed her fingertips over his mouth. "No more. We could spend all our todays on what-ifs, but instead we should be focused on now. There is no guarantee for the future. All we have is this minute, and I for one want to relish it. We don't get do-overs in life."

He nodded and pressed his mouth to the sensitive spot in the hollow of her neck. "I do love you, Annie Grace."

"I've always loved you, Lincoln Cooper, and I love you more today, but less than tomorrow."

He scooped up the basket and took the blanket from her as they walked to where the UTV was parked. She sat in the middle of the bench seat and Linc held her close to his side as they slowly drove home.

Annie looked at the stars above them and her land stretched out for as far as the eye could see and beyond. Second chances were precious and no matter what, she'd fight for what she wanted. And someday, she'd marry this man sitting next to her. They might not be blessed with children, but they'd have love and a life together.

She kissed his cheek.

"What was that for?"

Her heart sighed in her chest, and she traced the outline of his jaw with feather-like kisses.

He laughed. "That tickles."

"We've got a second chance with our first love. Not many people get that."

He stopped driving. "I'll spend the rest of my days thankful that we have a second chance."

She snuggled closer to his body. "I'll bet Pops is smiling down on us."

He laughed. "Are you kidding? He'll be saying it's about darn time." He took his foot off the brake and eased them forward.

She looked up at the heavens and blinked back the tears that threatened to leak out of her eyes and whispered, "Thanks, Pops, for everything."

Chapter Twenty-Two

In the two short weeks Daphne had been gone, Linc watched the whirlwind known as Annie make things happen. She had hired an architect who would be at the ranch the day after tomorrow. Daphne was moving to Montana, and it was official as soon as she and Annie returned from the airport.

Linc glanced up and shielded his eyes as the quad cab ranch truck sped down the long gravel drive, leaving a wake of dust billowing up. There was only one person who ever drove like that—Annie. His heart soared with anticipation of seeing her and officially welcoming Daphne to ranch life. Things were certainly not going to be the same ole routine with these ladies on the property.

He waited under the portico as the truck came to a stop and Annie grinned at him from behind the wheel. He walked around to her door and pulled it open, giving her a lingering kiss before noticing the bags in the back of the truck bed.

His eyes grew wide. "Is this all she has?"

"Not by a long shot." Annie laughed. "The rest is coming by truck. Do you think we can find some space to store her furniture in one of the barns? She has some she didn't want to leave behind."

Daphne walked around the back of the truck. "Hey, Linc, don't worry. The moving truck won't be here for at least a month so I might have even found a place to live by then."

He watched a flicker of annoyance flash over Annie's face and saw the glint in her eyes. He knew that look and Daphne was about to discover just how stubborn her friend could be on certain matters. In a surprising twist, she had held her tongue.

"Good news. I picked out a horse for you. Don't worry. She's gentle and good with new riders."

"I don't need one just for me." Daphne glanced at Annie. "Do I?"

With a quick lift of her shoulder, Annie said, "Since riding horses is a way of life and the best way to see everything about the new resort would be from the saddle, like the guests, you need a horse. And Linc will find someone to give you some pointers on taking care of your horse."

Her eyebrow shot up. "I have to take care of a horse? I can barely take care of me."

"There are a few things you'll need to do, but it's not hard. The ranch hands will take care of mucking the stall and feeding her." Linc grabbed two large suitcases and then handed two smaller ones to the ladies. "I'll come back for the last two."

After depositing the suitcases in Daphne's room, Annie was waiting for him in the hall. "Do you have time for coffee? Mary's whipped up some cinnamon muffins." She slid her arms around his waist before laying her head on his chest. "It's so good to have Daphne here, but I just don't understand why she's anxious to get her own place. The house is huge and it's not like she won't have privacy; she has an entire wing to herself."

"I'm sure once she's settled in, you'll have the chance to talk and figure out what will be best."

She held him tighter. "This is nice." His stomach grumbled and she laughed. "Guess I should get you a couple of muffins." She tipped her head back and smiled and he kissed her.

"What time is the architect coming?"

"Tomorrow at nine. This afternoon I'm going to walk Daphne around and explain what I'm thinking, get her input to see if it will flow for ac-tivities and meals."

"Want some company?" He steered her to the kitchen and poured her a mug of coffee while she took a seat at the table.

"If you changed your mind and want to be around when the architect comes out, that'd be great, but this afternoon we'll be fine."

"The horse I picked for her is a gentle mare named Misty. I put her in the stall next to Bowie."

"We'll swing by and spend some time with them. How's Beau doing?"

"The colt is doing fantastic. There's a bright future with him. He's smart and curious, loves to be around people, and doesn't seem to shy away from anything. I just started to introduce the halter to him."

She gave him a quizzical look. "Isn't that a little late?"

He set the mugs on the table and took the plate of muffins from the counter for them. "There are different thoughts on when it's best to introduce it, but I like the slower approach. It will give him time to build up trust with me. I try to spend time with him every day, and Bowie of course."

She said, "Now that I'm settled, I plan on doing the same and we need to talk about how many horses we'll need for the resort. We'll need to add on to the horse stable for the resort guests, and I'm serious about breeding quarter horses."

He nodded. "You're serious about expanding into horses and not just being a cattle ranch?" He stirred his coffee and was reminded how much he admired her mind; it was working to plan for a long-term future.

"Yes, as long as we can devote the proper resources to each offshoot of the ranch, we'll have several revenue streams. Diversification is the key to being sustainable long term. Which brings me to another area, making the ranch more self-sustaining. I'm not sure how we achieve less of a carbon footprint, but when the architect is here, I'm going to ask for recommendations on any consultants who might be able to work with us."

"Lofty goals but try to take on one project at a time unless they're directly linked."

She patted his hand. "I work best when my brain has different projects at various phases to ponder."

"You're so much like Pops."

She took a sip of her coffee and her eyes sparkled over the rim. "Do you think I'm overly ambitious?"

"More like driven."

Mary walked into the kitchen and gave them both a warm smile. "Now, this is what I like to see —my two favorite people talking over coffee."

"Thanks for the muffins." Linc held one up. "They're delicious." He got up and said, "Join us and I'll get you a mug."

Mary sat next to Annie. "Daphne is unpacking. I'm so happy she's staying with us; this big house has been way too quiet."

Linc watched Mary as she spoke. Her happiness shone clear in her eyes. He handed her the mug.

"Linc, I could get used to you being around more too." Now there was a mischievous twinkle in her eyes. "Even with you tromping around in your work boots." It was just like her to poke fun at him.

He felt the heat flush his cheeks at the gentle rebuke about taking off his shoes. "I'll work on taking my boots off or just staying in the kitchen, and if you keep feeding me, you know I'll always be around."

She glanced at Annie. "I think you have more than my cooking to encourage you to join us."

Annie's face grew a sweet shade of pink. She opened her mouth and then closed it.

"I do have incentive." He grinned at Annie

and then Mary. "But now, I have work to do. There's baling to plan for and so much more."

"Dinner tonight?" Annie looked at him. "We can go to The Lucky Bucket. When I drove through town, I saw there's a band tonight."

"That sounds like fun, and Daphne needs to come with us. She can meet some of the locals. Mary, are you interested?"

With a wave of her hand, she said, "No, thank you, but have fun, and if anyone is up for breakfast in the morning, it'll be ready about seven."

Before Linc could answer, Annie said, "We'll be there and are you taking requests?" She winked at him. "Huckleberry pancakes? I'll pick some to help out."

"You have more than enough to do and there is a nice patch of them close by. I'll take a golf cart out to pick and freeze some too. The season will be gone before we know it."

Annie groaned. "You know how much I love them." She got up from the table and gently squeezed the older woman's shoulders.

Mary patted her hands. "Just like your daddy, they were his favorite berries too."

"What if we let everyone know about our plans tonight, invite anyone who wants to go, and it'll be on me. As a thank you for a good summer season."

Linc had never been surprised by the generosity of Pops, and Annie was following in his footsteps. "I'll spread the word but I'm picking you and Daphne up, and I'll be your designated driver."

"That's very sweet of you."

Daphne strolled into the kitchen. "What has your handsome boyfriend done now?" She grabbed a muffin and broke off a tiny piece.

He stood a little taller, liking that others recognized him as Annie's guy. "We're going out to The Lucky Bucket tonight. There's a band and I'm going to round up a bunch of us to go. I've offered to be the DD for you ladies."

She waved a hand in front of her. "You guys go. I'm bushed."

"Nonsense." Annie stood next to Linc and gave her a firm look. "You're coming with us; this isn't a date. You'll get to meet people and have some fun."

Daphne shrugged her shoulders. "Okay, as long as I'm not a third wheel."

He dropped a kiss on Annie's cheek. "I'll spread the word and I'm sure we'll have a good group."

"And I'll track down Polly and let her know too. It'll be a lot of fun." She gave him a slow, sexy wink. "Put on your dancing boots, Mr. Cooper, and I'll let you twirl me around the dance floor."

"I might step on your toes; it's been a while." Holding Annie in his arms while dancing held a strong appeal and it had been a while since they had. It was just one more thing to look forward to tonight.

At seven Linc parked the truck in front of the main house. A couple of times during the day, he caught glimpses of Annie and Daphne walking around with clipboards. It had been obvious they were on a mission and with the architect meeting mere hours away, preparation was key to not waste time or money. He ran up the front steps and tapped on the door before walking in.

Annie's smile filled her eyes and face which in turn warmed his heart. This was how life needed to be every day.

"Hi, handsome. We're almost ready to go."

"No rush." He kissed her and inhaled the spicy scent of her perfume, part woodsy and floral at the same time. Two sides of nature, two sides of the woman.

"Who all's coming tonight?" She snapped her fingers. "Polly will be there; she's going to meet us around eight."

"Clint and Quinn are coming out along with a few other guys, but some wanted me to pass along their thanks and asked for a rain check. Haying season is exhausting."

She nodded. "I guess I wasn't thinking when I came up with the idea."

"Never worry about being spur of the moment. Some of the best ideas happen when you don't overthink them." He took her hand and twirled her as if they were on the dance floor. "And it's something I love about you."

"You didn't used to. Remember the summer after high school when I wanted us to pack up and take the summer to travel up and down the West Coast? It was not your idea of a good time."

"I wouldn't say that, but I had just gotten hired to work for Pops that summer and if I wanted a permanent spot, it wouldn't have looked good to be traipsing around with you and then expect special favors for a job after the busiest season on a ranch. I needed to prove myself."

"Yeah, but you have to admit being a gypsy for a couple of months did hold a nice appeal."

He remembered that like it was yesterday and how badly he had wanted to go with her. Instead, he remained steady to his promise to work for her grandfather. "And I remember just to prove your point, you and Layne Roberts took off for a couple of weeks. I was a mess the entire time you were gone, and I don't think Pops was too happy either."

"At me or you?"

"Me. He thought I should have gone with you. As he put it, *I was a damn fool*." He thought for a minute at how prophetic those words were now. More times than he'd care to admit, he'd been a fool when it came to Annie, and even if he had to remind himself every day, he wasn't going to waste any more time.

He turned Annie to look directly at him and said, "I want to talk to you about something important."

She tipped her head. "What's wrong? All of a sudden you have the most serious expression."

"Nothing's wrong. It's just... I wanted to ask..."

"Annie." Daphne hurried into the room. "Can you tell me if I'm dressed okay? I'm not sure what to wear and don't want to stand out like the chick from Boston, if you catch my drift."

Her forward motion stopped when she looked from Linc to Annie. "Did I interrupt something?"

Annie looked at him. "Linc has something on his mind and was going to tell me what it was."

Not now he wasn't and who was he kidding? She needed romance for a proposal, not an off-the-cuff question as he dropped to one knee without a ring to seal the deal. He'd plan a quick trip to Bozeman for the perfect ring and then ask her to marry him.

"It can wait. It wasn't any big deal."

She gave him a questioning look. "Are you sure? And if it's confidential, Daphne can give us a few minutes."

Backing out of the room, she said, "Sure. Just let me know when you're ready to leave."

"We can talk another time. Let's take off. I'd like to get a table before the band starts."

Annie looked from Linc to Daphne. "You heard the man; we're hitting the dusty trail." She looked at her friend's outfit. "You look great, jeans and a blouse are always a safe bet." She looked at her feet and that's when Linc noticed she was wearing high heels.

Annie nodded to them. "Come on. You need a pair of boots. The floors in the Bucket are original to the building and you'll trip and break something the minute you walk in the door."

The ladies left the room and Linc sank to the bench in the foyer. Mary came in and looked around.

"The girls aren't ready yet?"

"Daphne needed boots; she was wearing heels that looked to be about four inches."

Mary shook her head and chuckled. "It'll take a while to get the city out of the girl, but she's gonna make a solid addition to our ranch family." She gave him a sharp look. "Speaking of which, when are you gonna make your move?"

He was going to play dumb and hopefully he was a good enough actor to pull it off. "Not sure where you're going with that question, Mary, but things are just perfect the way they are."

With a *tsk, tsk,* she moved down the hall.

He exhaled and knew that had been a close call. She only pulled out the *tsk, tsk* at very specific times. If she had probed just a little, he'd have spilled his guts.

Chapter Twenty-Three

Over coffee Annie and Daphne dissected all the shenanigans at The Lucky Bucket last night.

"I can't believe there were so many people coming out on a Thursday night to hear the band, and what a fun name—Jumping Fish." Annie nibbled on a banana while waiting for Mary to come into the kitchen. She had gotten up early, excited to meet with the architect, and for the first time in ages, she beat Mary to making coffee. She had all the fixings out for pancakes and was going to slide the bacon in the oven in five minutes, but she would leave the pancakes to Mary. She made them so light and fluffy; hers were best for clay pigeons and target practice.

"The band was good and the drummer was good-looking." Daphne laughed. "But don't worry. I have tunnel vision when it comes to the new business venture here. Have you decided what you're doing about the name?"

"Yeah. We're still a ranch first and foremost, so it will be Grace Star Ranch with the resort portion to have its own section on the website. Not as an afterthought, but to keep the businesses separate. Even though my goal is to create new revenue streams, the resort has to carry its own weight financially, and as the new manager, it will be your job to book the cabins and hold amazing events and dinners which means you'll need to work with Quinn."

"He's a pretty quiet guy. I don't think he'll appreciate me charging into his kitchen, telling him what to do."

"I think you'll actually need to hire an assistant for Quinn, someone who can help him feed not just the hands but also the guests. Give that some thought and if possible, I'd like to hire local folks. It's part of my plan to support the town too. I don't want any business owners thinking the resort will rob tourists from the restaurants or the B & B in town."

Daphne agreed and pulled a clipboard off the chair and placed it in front of Annie, who flipped through the pages and noted the events she wanted to hold when they opened. All were based on the seasons. "This looks well thought out for good weather—trail rides, bon fires, stargazing, and fishing—but what about winter? We get a lot of snow and there is so much to do."

"I've never been here in the winter months, so I plan on taking advantage of all the things that are in the area this year and make plans around them. It will take a little longer to get the website up to date with schedules, but I need to immerse myself in the area."

Intuitively, Annie had known Daphne was the perfect person to head up the resort and it made sense for events, but how would they be able to book guests if the website didn't have any information?

"I know that look." Daphne wagged her finger in Annie's direction. "How to conquer the world in three easy steps."

"It'll take more than that, but I guess some of this is unknown until we talk to the architect and find out how long it will take to build the cabins and open."

Linc strode in the side door. "Morning," he said and kissed her upturned face. "Plotting so early." He poured himself a mug of coffee and slid the tray of bacon into the oven and set the timer.

Annie watched and marveled at how at ease he was and that she didn't have to ask him to help out.

"Where's Mary? Are we making breakfast this morning?"

Her voice drifted down the hall. "I'm coming." She entered the room, then she grabbed the apron from the hook and tied it on. "What's gotten into all of you, up so early?"

"I couldn't sleep. I'm like a kid at Christmas,

getting ready to open presents, only we're talking about designs for the new guest cabins today."

With practiced ease, the older woman measured ingredients without consulting a recipe card or cookbook. It was like most things she cooked. Tears pricked Annie's eyes and she pushed back from the table and hurried into the living room. The tears slid down her face as it hit her like a ton of bricks. There was going to come a day when Mary would be gone and she'd have lost the final connection to her grandparents and her mom and dad. All of the special foods they had for holidays would be lost forever and traditions would end.

She could feel Linc behind her. He waited silently like a mighty oak tree, strong and unyielding. She leaned into his chest and he wrapped his arms around her as she let the tears flow, the dam broken. He never said a word but held her while sobs racked her body. Pops was gone and no matter what she did, she'd never be able to show him the changes she planned for the ranch. He'd never be able to tell her she was on the right track or making mistakes.

When she was left with nothing but soft hiccups, Linc pressed a handkerchief into her hand. "Use this to dry your tears."

She did and pointed to the small washroom around the corner. "I'm going to wash my face. I'll be right back."

"I'll wait for you."

She closed the door and inspected her blotchy face and bloodshot eyes and the end of her nose was red. That had been one ugly cry, the one that had eluded her during the funeral and the months since. What must Linc think of her?

She splashed cool water over her face and patted it dry with a thick dark-green towel. It was Pops' favorite color and it almost brought a fresh wave of tears. A light tap on the door made her call out, "I'll be right there."

When she opened the door, it was Mary on the other side. She took Annie's hand and led her out the front door to the bench.

The two women sat for several long minutes without speaking. Annie glanced at Mary who said, "Grief takes its time. There's no predicting when, why, or where it'll hit you. But I do know if you don't let it wash over you and deal with the pain from loss, it just waits and eventually it seeps out like it did today."

Annie hung her head and grasped Mary's hand like it was a lifeline. "I've lost everyone I love but you."

Quietly, she said, "Not everyone. Linc loves you with all his heart and Daphne didn't agree to move away from her home on a whim. She did it because of your friendship and she trusts you. And you have me too."

Her heart constricted. *But for how long?* She'd seen that Mary had slowed down, but that still wasn't something that she could say. Time wasn't on their side.

"Child, there is a time for everyone to leave this earth, but I have no plans to leave anytime soon."

She pulled Annie close and fresh tears slipped down her cheeks. She let the tears flow. At least this time it wasn't those deep sobs that came from her toes. The women sat and a red-winged blackbird perched on the top step and hopped closer to Annie before cocking its head from side to side.

"Look, it's Pops' favorite bird. He would have loved to have seen this little guy."

"Who's to say he can't see him or an even better thought, maybe he sent the bird to you, giving you a sense of peace."

That would be something Pops would do. He never wanted to see her cry and she had done a lot of that so far today. So much for dealing with her grief in a controlled manner. Then it dawned on her. There was no such thing. When her parents had died, she had cried for days on end, totally inconsolable, and when her grandmother and then Pops passed, she didn't allow herself to go down that same path.

The little bird continued to watch her, almost waiting for her to stop crying. She wiped her face with the hem of her shirt.

"It's time we go inside. You have a meeting to prepare for and I have pancakes to serve." She gave Annie a bear hug and then cupped her cheek. Looking deep in her eyes, she said, "Don't bury your feelings; it never works." Concern clouded Mary's eyes. "Promise me you'll try."

"Some habits are hard to change." She watched the little bird take flight. "But I'll find a way to make it happen."

They walked inside the house where Linc and Daphne were sitting at the table. The kitchen smelled of crispy bacon and coffee. She took a seat next to Linc and he never left her side while they had breakfast. Daphne kept the conversation light while they talked about simple things like favorite breakfast foods and desserts. After devouring the pancakes, Annie glanced at the clock and saw she had thirty minutes to get ready for her meeting. Her nerves fluttered in anticipation. In a few hours she'd have a clear picture of what her next steps would be.

Annie and Daphne were on the front porch waiting for Tasha Melnick. She had come highly recommended in the report Annie had memorized from Lucas Gasperini. She smiled to herself. If he had only known her real motivation to read the report. It was their intellectual property so she hadn't scanned it into her computer, but she did take copious notes and memorized a few key things, one being the list of top architects suitable for this type of project. She also memorized the first two general contractors, both of which their reputations proceeded them.

Daphne looked at her. "How can you be so composed when this meeting will change everything for both of us?"

She let the smile slide from one side of her face to the other. "That's exactly what I'm hoping for, to give you a solid reason to never leave Montana and to expand my business. I can't wait to see how this will launch us into the world of entrepreneurship. Maybe we'll have our own line of spa products, clothing, outdoor gear, and saddles." She laughed. "I have no idea, but the possibilities are endless."

"I know. It's exciting." Daphne wiped the palms of her hands on her jeans.

At least Annie had talked her out of wearing a business suit and heels. She still needed at least one if not two pairs of cowboy boots to really look the part. As far as Annie was concerned, if you looked like you belonged and treated people with respect and kindness, they'd accept you into the community, but of course Daphne would always add her own flair to anything she wore or did. Today she had wrapped a silk scarf around her throat and tucked it into the front of her blouse. A great way to add a touch of panache to her outfit.

A camel-colored Suburban was coming down the driveway and the rain from last night kept the dust down.

"I'm guessing that's Tasha"—she glanced at her watch—"and she's early. We're off to a promising start." Annie walked down the wide steps with Daphne by her side.

The woman stepped from her vehicle. She was tall and very thin with short no-nonsense blond hair and deep-brown assessing eyes. She was dressed in a black short-sleeve turtleneck, jeans, and fashionable work boots, suitable for walking around a jobsite. She came around the front of the truck and smiled, her hand extended to Annie.

"Hello, Annie." She looked at Daphne. "Tasha Melnick."

With a firm handshake, Annie said, "Nice to see you again and this is Daphne Brenner. She'll be running the day-to-day operations of the resort and I want her involved from the ground up."

Tasha shook her hand. "It's a pleasure, Daphne." She surveyed the land. "The ranch is stunning." She turned. "And you want to build guest cabins?"

"As we talked about on the phone, I was thinking of starting with six and I'd like to leave the possibility of expanding open."

"It's good you're not going all in, so you can first see how things work out." She placed a hand over her lips. "But you didn't hear that from me. My father, who owns the firm, would say go big right away."

Annie had liked this woman the first time they met and even more so now that she discovered Tasha wasn't out to line her pockets. They were going to work very well together.

"Tasha, I thought we'd take a golf cart around the buildings. I can show you what's here and what else I have in mind. Then we can look at where I think the cabins would be best suited. My ranch manager will join us at that point since this will impact the workings of our cattle and horse breeding programs." She gestured to the two golf carts at the edge of the drive. "We can leave your bags in the house or you can take them, your choice."

"I'll leave the bag and just bring my tablet if that's alright. I want to take pictures and notes so when I return to the office and begin the design phase, it will compliment what's already here."

Daphne took her leather tote bag and said, "I'll just put this inside and follow you."

Annie and Tasha walked in the direction of the golf carts. "I was surprised you wanted to expand your ranch and add the resort component. Do you mind if I ask why?"

"It's all about multilayered revenue streams. And I had a developer approach me about buying the ranch and although my plan isn't as grand, it opened my eyes to an opportunity."

She nodded. "I was sorry to hear about your grandfather. When I told my father I was coming out today, he had nothing but good things to say about Mr. Grace."

Annie swallowed the lump in her throat and pushed aside the sadness, then smiled. She had cried enough. "He was amazing and I think he'd be happy to know I was making my own mark on our family's land."

"I'm excited to be working with you. Mostly I deal with men, who can at times be stuck in the last century." She gave Annie a quick glance. "They're not all like that, but working with someone who shares similar life experiences, well, I think we can make this amazing, blend into the landscape, and not impact your ranch operation."

"That's important to me." Annie pointed to where the greenhouse was planned. "This year I hired a woman to run the gardens for the ranch. My goal is to grow more of our own food organically. We're building a greenhouse later this year. I had wanted to get started soon, but I'm running out of time to break ground."

"I love that idea." She looked over her shoulder. "If you don't mind, I'd like to see that too since that will impact my design as well."

Annie gestured to the fence. "Let's start there. I'll introduce you to Polly and maybe you'll have an idea on how to help it look less industrial and more resort friendly."

"I'd be happy to incorporate that into the plan." She waved her tablet in the air and grinned.

Annie opened the gate door to the gardens.

Chapter
Twenty-Four

Annie set the phone down and crossed to the glass office doors and stepped outside. She tipped her head back so the sun could warm her face. It had been a month since Tasha Melnick toured the ranch and she called to set up an appointment for tomorrow to review the plans she had for the cabins and even the greenhouse. Polly had confirmed the size of the greenhouse and also in a cheeky move, she suggested they go bigger to have more space to grow flowers for the ranch too. When Tasha had been there, she agreed with Linc's idea to plant trees to break the new access road with the back of the main house. But instead of one row, it was a zigzag pattern to give full and quick coverage, and somehow Linc managed to find a landscape company to get started. How that man moved mountains amazed her.

She heard the familiar sound of horse hooves coming from around the side of the house in the paddock that abutted the yard. She crossed to see what was going on and her heart ticked up its rhythm when she saw Linc riding Darby and Bowie was trailing behind him, saddled and ready for a ride.

"This is a surprise." She climbed the wooden fence and slipped over the top rail, then jumped down to scratch Bowie's nose. She murmured softly, "Hey, girl."

"Got time for a ride? I think Bowie is itching to hit the trail again."

She looked up at him. "What about Beau? Do you think he's okay without his momma?"

"We won't be gone long, and it would be good for him to spend a little time with Misty. She's become a surrogate mom." He laughed. "It'll be fine. Trust me?"

She gave him an assessing look. "Are you sure he'll be safe?"

"Annie, come on. Just follow my lead and trust me; it'll be fun."

She kissed Bowie's nose and patted her neck before putting her foot in the stirrup and swinging into the saddle. She glanced over at Linc. The way he sat a horse was heart thumping.

With light pressure of her calves on Bowie's sides and lifting the reins up and forward, they ambled at a leisurely pace with Darby falling in step.

"Have you noticed the trees are starting to pop out some early color?"

Linc leaned over and slipped the loop from the gate so they could ride through. He left it open for now and when they got back, he'd secure it. He touched the front of his shirt to double-check the chain he had around his neck was still there. Satisfied, he guided their mounts to the lower road. He was taking the long way around to the river and their spot.

"Tell me about the new construction project. Have you heard from Tasha yet?"

Annie tipped her head back and let the sun grace her face. Linc kept an eagle eye out just in case Bowie decided to pick up the pace and unseat her.

"She's coming out tomorrow. Want to be in the meeting and hear all the amazing things that will be happening?"

"Wild ponies couldn't keep me away."

She leveled her gaze at him. "You know, I really thought you'd fight me on the expansion of the ranch. You're more of a traditional cowboy."

He chuckled. "I do like tradition, but there's something to be said for change and moving in new directions. Besides, I think it's a great idea and I'm partial to how stunning our ranch is. If people want the dude ranch experience, this is the best place for them to get it."

He'd never readily admit he was taken off guard when Annie first mentioned the idea, but Pops had said to him that if you didn't change, the end result was extinction to a way of life and that was a fate he didn't want to have happen on Annie's watch.

Bowie eased into a slow trot and his mount did the same.

"I'm glad you brought her around to me. This is a nice break. My head was spinning with spreadsheet overload."

"Anything you want to talk about?" He'd be happy to have her bounce any ideas off him.

"I'm just running an analysis of feed that we'll need for the winter." She glanced over at him. "I know you provided me with a full report but analyzing data is what I do best, and it helps me to feel more connected to everything that goes on around here."

He had a moment of concern. Did she doubt his abilities? He shook that off. Everything that surrounded them was her responsibility and she needed to double-check any numbers she wanted.

"I welcome your review. So if you have any questions, just let me know." He pulled the reins to the side and the horse turned right, but they weren't going to their usual spot. He wanted to create a new memory for them.

"Where are we going?" Annie looked around. "I assumed we were headed to our spot at the river."

"We're almost there. I want to show you something, and then we'll head back to the house." He arranged for Clint to take care of the horses since he'd asked Mary to have champagne waiting so they could all celebrate together.

She sighed. "This was exactly what I needed—fresh air along with my favorite horse and man. This must be a little slice of heaven."

"I'm third on the list?" He stifled a laugh.

"Well"—the word came out in a long drawl—"all three are equal?" Her voice tipped up with the question that made her laugh. "You're first on this list but for the record Bowie is a very close second."

"Spoken like a true cowgirl, where your horse comes first."

Annie leaned over Bowie's neck and whispered into the mare's twitching ear. After a moment she straightened up. "I had to make sure Bowie didn't take offense to you edging her out by a nose."

The river was a ways off, but there was a large pine tree and a few small rocks, just large enough for them to sit on. He slid down from the saddle and secured the reins around a low tree limb and repeated the motion with Bowie's. Then he held out his arms and Annie slid into them.

"Let's relax before we head back."

She gave him a side-eye and held his hand while they crossed to the sun-warmed rocks. "It's beautiful here." She pulled him down next to her and leaned into his side. "Make sure from time to time you pull me out of the office so we can have these mini adventures."

He kissed the top of her head. "So I can rescue you from paperwork whenever I want?"

"Within reason." She snuggled into the crook of his arm.

Now that they were here, the words he had thought would come easy were lodged in his throat. She didn't seem to suspect a thing which was good; it was buying him some time.

"I wish we had a fishing pole. Fresh trout for dinner would hit the spot."

"Next time I'll remember poles." He perched

his hat back on his head and cleared his throat. He'd better speak up before she suggested it was time to head back to the house.

"A while back, before Pops got real sick, he called me to the main house, said he needed to have a serious talk with me."

She looked up at him. "I'm glad you were there for him. He loved you like a son."

"I think he knew the feeling was mutual, not the son part but that I considered him family." He attempted to keep the quiver out of his voice. "During this conversation, he point blank asked me why I never found a woman to share my life with. He knew all along why we really had broken up and although he respected our privacy, he wasn't happy about it."

"I think that made three of us." She was quiet, letting him do most of the talking.

"I knew he deserved an answer and that's when I told him I was a one-woman kind of man and I messed up and sent the only woman I'd ever loved away."

She sat up and placed a hand on his cheek. "Linc, we've been over all of this and we've gotten past it. There's no sense rehashing it all again."

"Sweetheart, let me get this off my chest. I promise I'm getting somewhere; it's just taking me a little longer."

She shifted on the rock and took his hand. "I'm listening."

That just ramped his nerves off the charts. But he kissed the top of her hand and looked into her beautiful blue eyes. "So he asked me straight up if I loved you why hadn't I told you and found a way to fix things between us. At the time I didn't have the courage to lay my heart on the line. No matter how much I wanted to, I let fear control my actions, and when you came back, I knew it was my chance, not just to make amends but, if I was very fortunate, to have a different future, with you."

He stood up from the rock and dropped to one knee. Tossing his hat aside, he withdrew the chain from around his neck.

"I know it hasn't been that long since you've learned the truth, but we both know time is precious so here goes..." He took the ring from the chain and held it at the tip of her fourth finger on her left hand.

"Annie Grace. I have loved you from the first time I laid eyes on you and your face is the only one I've ever wanted to wake up to for all the days of my life. Would you do me the honor of becoming my wife? We'll lasso life and live it to the max, loving under the sun, moon, and stars, and I promise that I'll be the husband you deserve."

She was blinking away the tears that clung to her lashes and she didn't say a word. His heart thudded in his chest. Had he missed his chance with her or worse, was he rushing her now, proposing before she was ready? He didn't move from bended knee. He would stay in this position until she said yes or no. As time slowed, his heartbeat stopped. Was she about to break his heart?

She sat on his bent leg and wrapped her arms around his neck. "Are you sure? I'm hardheaded or snarky and impetuous a lot of the time and I'm not going to change."

He cocked his head and the smile started on one side of his face and slid to the other. "Is that a yes?"

She pressed her mouth to his and whispered, "I loved you then, I love you now, and I'll love you forever." She wiggled her ring finger, urging him to slip the round diamond solitaire on her finger. Once it was in place, she looked deep into his eyes. "Yes, I'll be your wife."

In one smooth motion, he stood them up and twirled her in his arms. "I love you, Annie."

Epilogue

THE FOLLOWING SPRING

The snow was finally melting in the bright April sun. Annie stood on the back deck off her bedroom and watched Linc working Beau on the lead rope. She kept in the shadow of the house so he couldn't see her. It would never do for the groom to see the bride before the wedding.

Mary came up next to her. "Are you ready to get your hair and makeup done? Everyone is set up in the room next to Daphne's."

"Can you believe we're getting married today? I wish Pops could have walked me down the aisle."

Mary withdrew a small box and a creamy square envelope from behind her back. "Open this."

She gave Mary a small smile. "You didn't need to get me a gift."

"It's not from me. It's from Pops and there's a note too." She left the room and Annie dropped down into Pops' old leather armchair. It was a good thing she hadn't gotten her makeup done yet; this wasn't going to be easy. She was sorely missing Pops as well as her grandmother and parents today.

She tore open the envelope first and a notecard was inside.

My dear Annie,

Today is your wedding day to Linc and I couldn't be prouder of you both. I never gave up that you would find your way back to each other. He is your North Star and together you'll always be home. The item in the box is made up of pieces from your parents and grandparents. I love you, my darling girl. Be happy. Pops

She flipped open the top on the leather box and lying inside was a gold necklace with a diamond in the middle circle surrounded by rubies. She closed her eyes tight, remembering her mom's engagement ring was a diamond and rubies.

She flew down the hall. "Mary!"

She stepped into the hallway from the living room. "What is it, child?"

She held up the necklace. "Pops said this was made up of other jewelry. Do you know what was used?"

She nodded slowly and took a close look at the pendant. "Your grandmother's diamond is in the middle; the stones from your mother's engagement ring surround that, and the gold is from Pops', Pippa's, your parents, and even my wedding bands. This way we will always be close to your heart."

She threw her arms around Mary and held her tight as if her family were there too. "He always knew, didn't he?"

"He had hope and he believed in love." She kissed Annie's cheek. "Go freshen up. We have a wedding to get ready for. The car will be here soon and you can't be late."

"Thank you, Mary, for everything."

The older woman's eyes filled with happy tears. "Go."

Mary turned her around and pointed her to her bedroom, which after today would be hers and Linc's. Annie floated down the hall.

Annie stood in the vestibule of the church which was full of friends ready to celebrate the wedding over twenty years in the making. Clint made his way up the aisle to where she waited. He kissed her cheek.

"When Linc sees you, his eyes are gonna pop out of his head."

"Thank you, Clint. Does this mean we're almost ready to start?" The front door opened and Polly hurried in.

"Sorry I'm late." The words rushed out.

Annie noticed color flushed Clint's cheeks all the way to the tips of his ears. Now this was interesting and a good distraction to quell the butterflies in her stomach.

"You haven't missed a thing." She took Clint's hand. "Will you escort Polly to a seat?"

He took her hand and tucked it into the crook of his arm. "Of course." Polly dropped her eyes and gave him a shy smile.

Annie made a mental note to see what was going on when she and Linc got back from their honeymoon. They were going to Boston and then Cape Cod. She wanted to share every part of her life with him and what better way to do that than go to the East Coast.

Mary appeared at her elbow. "Now stop your matchmaking long enough to marry your handsome cowboy who is chomping at the bit at the altar."

"How do you know he's nervous?" She let Mary adjust her wide-brimmed hat and her pendant.

"I just checked in on him. Are you ready to take your last walk as a single woman?"

She nodded, not sure if the words would come out. Mary took her arm and they stepped to the closed double doors. The music changed and they eased open. Annie took her first step down the aisle and Linc moved to where they'd meet in front of the altar. He extended his hand and Mary placed her hand in his.

They stood in front of the pastor. Annie leaned over and whispered in Linc's ear.

"I broke the news to Bowie; you're officially in the number one spot for me."

With a hearty chuckle, he said, "Annie Grace, you've always been the only woman for me too."

The pastor said, "We are gathered here today to join Annie Grace and Lincoln Cooper."

Annie's heart was overflowing with love for this man holding her hand. She fell in love with him under the stars, and Lincoln Cooper was her North Star.

***

If you loved Stars Over Montana help other readers find this book: **Please leave a review now!**

Are you ready to read more about the Cowboys of River Junction? Order Hiding in Montana, book 2. Also don't forget to sign up for my newsletter for a free download at www.lucindarace.com/newletter

is a long-distance relationship their only option for their second chance?

The Sandy Bay Series
Sundaes on Sunday
A widowed school teacher and the airline pilot whose little girl is determined to bring her daddy and the lady from the ice cream shop together for a second chance at love.

Last Man Standing/Always a Bridesmaid
Barrett
Has the last man standing finally met his match?

Marie *May 2023*
Career focused city girl discovers small town charm can lead to love.

The Crescent Lake Winery Series
Breathe
Her dream come true may be the end of his...
Crush
The first time they met was fleeting, the second time restarted her heart.
Blush

He's always loved her but he left and now he's back...the question, does she still love him?

Vintage

He's an unexpected distraction, she gets his engine running...

Bouquet

Sweet second chances for a widow and the handsome billionaire...

Holiday Romance

The Sugar Plum Inn

The chef and the restaurant critic are about to come face to face.

Last Chance Beach

Shamrocks are a Girl's Best Friend

Will a bit of Irish luck and a matchmaking uncle give Kelly and Tric a chance to find love?

A Dickens Holiday Romance

Holiday Heart Wishes

Heartfelt wishes and holiday kisses...

Holly Berries and Hockey Pucks

Hockey, holidays, and a slap shot to the heart.

Christmas in July
She's the hometown girl with the hometown advantage. Right?

A Secret Santa Christmas
Christmas just isn't Holly's thing, but will a family secret help her find the true meaning of Christmas?

It's Just Coffee Series 2020
The Matchmaker and The Marine
She vowed never to love again. His career in the Marines crushed his ability to love. Can undeniable chemistry and a leap of faith overcome their past?

The MacLellan Sisters Trilogy
Old and New
An enchanted heirloom wedding dress and a letter change three sisters lives forever as they fulfill their grandmothers last request try on the dress.
Borrowed
He's just a borrowed boyfriend. He might also be her true love.
Blue

Will an enchanted wedding dress work its magic one more time?

The Loudon Series

<u>Between Here and Heaven</u>

Ten years of heaven on earth dissolved in an instant for Cari McKenna when her husband Ben died.

<u>Lost and Found</u>

Love never ends... A widow who talks to her late husband and her handsome single neighbor who has secretly loved her for years.

<u>The Journey Home</u>

Where do you go to heal your heart? You make the journey home...

<u>The Last First Kiss</u>

When life handed Kate lemons, she baked.

<u>Ready to Soar</u>

Kate will fight for love, won't she?

<u>Love in the Looking Glass</u>

Will Ellie's first love be her last or will she become a ghost like her father?

<u>Magic in the Rain</u>

Dani's plan of hiding in plain sight may not have been the best idea.

Cozy Mystery Books
A Bookstore Cozy Mystery Series 2023
Books & Bribes
It was an ordinary day until the book of Practical Magic conked Lily on the head causing her to see stars. And then she discovered her cat, Milo, could talk.

Catnip & Crimes
Tea & Trouble
Scares & Dares

Social Media

Follow Me on Social Media

Like my Facebook page
Join Lucinda's Heart Racer's Reader Group on
Facebook
Twitter @lucindarace
Instagram @lucindaraceauthor
BookBub
Goodreads
Pinterest

About the Author

Award-winning and best-selling author Lucinda Race is a lifelong fan of reading. As a young girl, she spent hours reading novels and getting lost in the fun and hope they represent. While her friends dreamed of becoming doctors and engineers, her dreams were to become a writer—a novelist.

As life twisted and turned, she found herself writing nonfiction but longed to turn to her true passion. After developing the storyline for A McKenna Family Romance, it was time to start living her dream. Her fingers practically fly over computer keys as she weaves stories of mystery and romance.

Lucinda lives with her two little dogs, a miniature long hair dachshund and a shih tzu mix rescue, in the rolling hills of western Massachusetts. When she's not at her day job, she's immersed in her fictional worlds. And if she's not writing romance or cozy mystery novels, she's reading everything she can get her hands on.